The Distant Sound of Boiling Tea

a screenplay

Also by Michael-Patrick Harrington

Deep Autumn

I See No Angels

Saving Magdalene

Sweater Girl and Other Tales of Mondauk County

www.michaelpatrickharrington.com

The Distant Sound of Boiling Tea

Michael-Patrick Harrington

Published by Silk Raven Press
a division of Mondauk Enterprises Inc.
PO Box 31, Ambler, PA 19002

SILK
RAVEN
PRESS

(SRP-005)

The Distant Sound of Boiling Tea
ISBN: 0692444580
ISBN-13: 9780692444580

WGAE registration# I215312

Cover art by Nichole Kohler

Cover designed by Pepper Lillie
www.pepperlillie.com

As always, mere thanks doesn't cover it for Beth Meier,
who waded through my words
and helped me find the diamonds in the mud—again.

Much gratitude to:
Nichole Kohler,
who created the cover artwork,
and
Dominique Messihi & Steven Brandsdorfer
of Pepper Lillie,
who designed the cover

Thank you to
Professor Larry Loebell
and everyone who participated in
the Play and Screenwriting Workshop
at Arcadia University, Spring '10, especially:
Abby Grosslein, my partner in crime,
and
Mary DeCarlo, who brought Ruth to life

I would be lost without my
booking agent, Kathleen Rose Harrington,
and my personal assistant/road manager, Kathie Cronk

Grātiās vōbīs agō:
Harleysville Books
Doylestown Bookshop
Mt. Airy Read & Eat
Farley's Bookshop
Big Blue Marble Bookstore

Acknowledgements

I am extremely grateful to the following people who patiently responded to my queries during the research process:

Jill Fertel,
Assistant District Attorney,
Philadelphia, PA

Marigold McCartney,
a former TPA Director of Operations

Kelly Stengel, MS, CRNP

Detective James A. Weiss,
Philadelphia Police Department,
my technical advisor

and
a kind and accommodating clergyman
who gave me his time and shared his knowledge
but wished to remain anonymous

Dedicated to my sister Kathie.
Even when we were little, you were a pillar of strength.
Regardless of blood, you are my loyal friend.
Sorry about the time I declared war on you and your room.

Soundtrack:

1. Moondance by Van Morrison
2. Superman by R.E.M.
3. Rainy Day Women #12 & 35 by Bob Dylan
4. Welcome to Paradise by Green Day
5. Pour Some Sugar on Me by Def Leppard
6. Do You Hear What I Hear? by Bob Dylan
7. Mustang Sally by Wilson Pickett
8. Into the Mystic by Van Morrison
9. Baby, Please Don't Go by Them
10. Have I Told You Lately by Van Morrison
11. Brown Eyed Girl by Van Morrison
12. Mannish Boy by Muddy Waters & the Band
13. Caravan by Van Morrison & the Band
14. Maggie Mae by Rod Stewart
15. Stephanie Says by the Velvet Underground
16. Hot for Teacher by Van Halen
17. And It Stoned Me by Van Morrison
18. Father Figure by George Michael
19. That's What Friends are For by Dionne & Friends
20. 50 Ways to Leave Your Lover by Paul Simon
21. Lithium by Nirvana
22. Hit the Road Jack by Ray Charles
23. Free Fallin' by Tom Petty
24. Take Me Back by Van Morrison

So dark a mind within me dwells,
   And I make myself such evil cheer,
That if *I* be dear to some one else,
   Then some one else may have much to fear;
But if *I* be dear to some one else,
   Then I should be to myself more dear.

Alfred Lord Tennyson, "Maud"

The Distant Sound of
Boiling Tea

FADE IN:

EXT. RUTH'S HOUSE – NIGHT (DUSK)

A single, middle class house on a clean, tree-lined street. A newspaper—the *Mondauk Common*—flutters against the railing. The lawn is littered with leaves. The neighbors' lawns are raked.

> RUTH (V.O.)
> William Gladstone wrote, "If you are cold, tea will warm you. / If you are too heated, tea will cool you. / If you are too depressed, tea will cheer you. / If you are too exhausted, tea will calm you."

INT. RUTH'S HOUSE – KITCHEN – NIGHT (DUSK)

Somewhat cluttered. A stainless steel tea kettle begins to whistle loudly just as someone knocks at the front door. An empty saucepan sits on the adjacent unlit burner.

> RUTH (V.O.)
> This little poem always reminds me of cozy things you can look forward to because you know they're waiting for you at the end of a long, cold day. The whistle of a boiling tea kettle is one of those things. It's like the comforting sound of a train whistle you hear in the distance before you fall asleep.

INT. RUTH'S HOUSE – LIVING ROOM – NIGHT (DUSK)

RUTH ST. CLAIR, 36, bounds down the stairs into the living room. She is attractive with dirty blonde hair but often dresses down, as if trying her best not to look like she tries. Ruth stops to straighten a small framed picture of herself with her husband Phil and her son Danny before heading towards the kitchen and the whistling kettle.

> RUTH
> Phil! Phil, can you get the door? Danny! Danny, can you answer the—

The knocking becomes more insistent. The doorbell rings.

                              RUTH (CONT'D)
Coming!
                    (to herself as she walks to the door)
          Please be an eager Girl Scout hawking Thin Mints out of
          season. I already have this month's *Watchtower*.

She quickly looks into the entranceway mirror. As she opens the door, a
Halloween skeleton decoration taped to the front falls off.

EXT. LISA ANN'S HOUSE – DAY

There are Thanksgiving decorations on the doors and windows of a few
neighboring houses, but not this one. LISA ANN KAVANAGH, 34, pretty
with long black hair, moves past a group of reporters huddled around her
low iron gate as she makes her way to the backdoor. The reporters shout
questions. One voice rises above the rest.

                         FEMALE REPORTER
               What will you do now, Mrs. Kavanagh?

Lisa Ann wearily turns around.

                      FEMALE REPORTER (CONT'D)
               What else can—

                            LISA ANN
                        (her face drawn)
          What else is there? Nothing. There *was* nothing else.

INT. RUTH'S HOUSE – BASEMENT – NIGHT

It is dark. The basement door is slowly opened a crack. A Van Morrison
CD competes with the sounds of Christmas carolers outside and two
women conversing on the other side of the door.

INT. RUTH'S HOUSE – KITCHEN – NIGHT

The tea kettle is whistling. A gun goes off. Water spills from a ragged hole
in the kettle, hissing as it hits the flames. The empty saucepan crashes to the
floor. Screaming replaces the whistling.

INT. RUTH'S HOUSE – LIVING ROOM – NIGHT (DUSK)

As the kettle continues to whistle, Ruth bends down to pick up the Halloween decoration but stops. Standing on her steps are COTTEN, a plainclothes detective in his late 40s and CAROL, a middle-aged woman wearing a jacket with a Mondauk County Child Welfare Services patch. They are accompanied by a uniformed Mondauk Proper police officer.

> RUTH
> I knew it was a little early for trick or treating. Jesus. What did my husband do now? He actually pee *on* a stripper this time rather than—

> DETECTIVE COTTEN
> (showing his badge)
> Ruth St. Clair?

> CAROL
> (as Ruth is nodding)
> We need to talk to you and your husband. It's about your son. It's about Danny.

EXT./INT. LISA ANN'S HOUSE – LIVING ROOM – NIGHT

The leaves on the trees have just started to turn. Through the curtainless bow windows, a party is in progress. Lisa Ann, smiling, serves a man a drink. When she bends over to change the CD, he playfully smacks her behind. A nearby couple laughs. Other people huddle in circles. Many are smoking.

PAUL, 54, sits in a lounge chair miserably staring into his drink as Lisa Ann starts dancing and singing to "Moondance."

INT. PHIL'S CAR – NIGHT

Ruth's husband, PHIL, 37, unshaven and unkempt, sits in his car drinking a can of beer, watching Lisa Ann's performance.

INT. MARCIE'S HOUSE – LIVING ROOM – NIGHT

MARCIE DIETLIN, 61, wearing a full-length nightgown and a thick robe, watches Lisa Ann's party through a pair of binoculars. Marcie's house is across a side street from Lisa Ann's. Still spying, she dials the phone. Strains of "Moondance" are in the background.

>   MARCIE
> Addie Mae, can you hear—
>   (beat)
> Carson isn't on TV anymore.
>   (beat)
> No, I don't know what they did with Doc Severinsen. Just
> listen to this.

Marcie holds the receiver up to the window.

INT./EXT. LISA ANN'S HOUSE – NIGHT

As "Moondance" comes to an end amid applause, Paul walks out to the back porch and stares at the stars. A few moments later, Lisa Ann joins him, a little out of breath. He points to the sky and traces a pattern.

>   PAUL
> Cassiopeia, remember?

>   LISA ANN
> How could I forget? Not many girls can say they lost their
> virginity to their astronomy professor in the university
> observatory.

>   PAUL
>   (still looking at the sky)
> Vain, jealous, petty Cassiopeia. Never without a hand
> mirror. I always thought her punishment was perhaps the
> best punishment ever for a bully.

>   LISA ANN
> How so?

She mouths the chorus of the song playing inside—"I am, I am, I am Superman, and I can do anything"—and begins slowly dancing somewhat suggestively, as if she can't help it.

PAUL
Well, in some books, Cassiopeia promised her daughter, the comely Andromeda, to Perseus. He'd rescued the girl from a sea serpent meant for her mother, who'd boasted of the family's beauty to the wrong Nereid.

LISA ANN
Maybe she thought she was hanging with a Siren.

PAUL
Cassiopeia became taken with Perseus, but he only had eyes for her daughter, so mom planned a nuptial ambush. Perseus, however, had recently slain Medusa, and he used her head to turn his assailants to stone. Poseidon was so incensed at Cassiopeia that he placed her in the heavens so that she would spend half the year upside down—the bully now forever a target.

LISA ANN
(leaning on Paul)
You think I'm vain, jealous, and petty? A sexual bully?

PAUL
(moving away)
You're not anything like the person I married.

LISA ANN
I was twenty-years-old then, Paul. I couldn't even buy beer.

PAUL
But you could vote. You have to give me that.

LISA ANN
You were cruising lecture halls, not senior proms. Exams not recess, remember?
(after an awkward moment of silence)
I know you just found an apartment, but you can always stay in the spare room until the end of the semester if you need to. Save a few ducats.

PAUL
Lisa Ann, we both know you're more than a little buzzed.

>   (beat)
> I'm aware of how small towns can be, especially one in
> Mondauk County. I don't mind being September's window
> dressing. I don't mind pretending tonight for your faculty
> friends. Hell, I haven't even told my mother yet. It's only a
> six month lease, so maybe I can win you back before
> finals.

>   LISA ANN
> I'm not going to be buzzed forever and neither are you.
> C'mon, Paul, we both know that going our separate ways is
> the right thing.

>   PAUL
> You used to look up to me, but once we got on the same
> footing—

>   LISA ANN
> We've never been equals. I just got tired of being on the
> bottom.

She rubs his arm briefly then heads towards the door.

>   PAUL
> You've sang better "Moondances," you know.

>   LISA ANN
>   (over her shoulder as she enters
>   the house)
> Not with clothes on.

INT. LISA ANN'S HOUSE – LIVING ROOM – NIGHT

The music is turned up. Everyone sings along with "Rainy Day Women #12 & 35." Paul is conspicuously absent.

INT. MARCIE'S HOUSE – LIVING ROOM – NIGHT

Marcie is on the phone again. Her husband, HAROLD, 65, sits at a small table tinkering with an HO scale train engine. The party and Dylan rumble in the background.

HAROLD

Can't we just go to bed, Marcie? They're not hurting anyone. Someone's going to see you with those binoculars, and you'll be the one—

MARCIE

Harold, shush!
(into the phone)
What do you mean which side of the street? Can't you hear—

FEMALE POLICE OPERATOR (V.O.)

If the house is on the north side of Highland Avenue, then it's still in the town of Mondauk Proper, and I'll dispatch a patrol car. But if it's on the south side, that's actually Rhawnhurst Borough, and you'll need to call their precinct.

MARCIE

I'm *on* the north side! The Dietlins!

HAROLD

You're on the North Pole. That's where you are, dear.

FEMALE POLICE OPERATOR (V.O.)

So the party's at your house?

MARCIE

How could the party be at our house?

HAROLD

A party? Could you imagine the horror?

FEMALE POLICE OPERATOR (V.O.)

How many people do you have there?

MARCIE

It's not at…I don't have any…I'm alone.

HAROLD

And I'm chopped liver. How d'ya do?

FEMALE POLICE OPERATOR (V.O.)

So they locked you out?

MARCIE
No one locked me out! I'm in my nightgown!

HAROLD
They could arrest you just for that.

FEMALE POLICE OPERATOR (V.O.)
Ma'am, I would advise you to put some clothes on. The
temperature—

MARCIE
(out of breath)
Highland...across the way...loud party...

FEMALE POLICE OPERATOR (V.O.)
Which side of the street, ma'am?

INT. PHIL'S CAR – NIGHT

Phil finishes a beer, tosses the can out the window, and takes off as a police
siren sounds in the distance.

INT. FATHER HOSKINS HIGH – CLASSROOM #1 – DAY

A Roman Catholic high school. Lisa Ann's social studies class. The students
are dressed in navy blue and white. DANNY ST. CLAIR, 15, a towheaded
boy with beatific looks, raises his hand. MEGAN RILEY rolls her eyes and
kicks the seat of PEGGY RUNYON, who sits in front of her. Danny is
clearly uncomfortable and stammers a bit.

DANNY
We study, um, we study women's issues because...because
women have the same right to be happy as men do, but
they have to fight for it. They, uh, they have to jump
through more hoops.

Megan titters, makes a circle with one hand, and moves an index finger in
and out of it as she whispers to Peggy.

MEGAN
That's Danny St. Clair's idea of a Kavanagh hoop.

Danny glares at Megan, looking ready to defend Lisa Ann.

> LISA ANN
> (considering Danny with amused
> curiosity)
> He speaks! Although that's not the only reason why we
> study women's issues, you're right, Danny. And the hoops
> keep getting smaller.
> (to Megan)
> Something geometric to add, Miss Riley? No? Good.
> Remember: you're not at the dinner table.

Megan slumps in her seat.

> LISA ANN (CONT'D)
> (to the class)
> What would Mr. Bogle say?
> (in a nasally voice)
> "You're sophomores! Act accordingly!"
> (as the giggling dies down)
> Now, if we turn to page…

INT. FATHER HOSKINS HIGH – LOCKER ROOM – DAY

Danny stuffs his books into a locker. There is a worn Green Day sticker on
the inside of the door. He is with two friends his age, COLIN and
TOMMY. Beefy, disheveled BRENDAN BAAR walks up and smacks
Colin on the back of his head.

> COLIN
> Cut it out, Brendan.

> BRENDAN
> Don't be a pussy, Colin.
> (pushing Danny into his locker door)
> Ah, another school year, another ten months to stare at
> Kavanagh's legs, huh, Danny Boy? Like a squirrel in
> reverse, storing enough spank bank material for the
> summer.

Danny pushes him back.

> BRENDAN (CONT'D)
> Hey, still involves nuts. Am I right, Tommy?

Tommy flinches and Danny pushes Brendan again.

> BRENDAN (CONT'D)
> Touchy about your girl, are ya? Well, did I tell you I saw Mrs. Kavanagh in her swimsuit at the Fox Rox pool this summer? Yeah, she had all these pubes sticking out of her—

Danny punches him. Brendan smiles and wipes away blood from his nose.

> BRENDAN (CONT'D)
> Funny. No one told me it was Beat the Geek Week. This is gonna be so much fun.

Tommy and Colin step aside as Brendan whales on Danny. A cute, tomboyish girl, CASEY GRACE, 15, wearing the jeff cap that she is rarely without, watches for a moment then runs down the hall to grab a teacher.

EXT. PUBLIC LIBRARY – DAY

Ruth exits the library with a stack of books and literally runs into FATHER DAVE, 45, the red-headed pastor of Assumption of Our Lady parish.

> FATHER DAVE
> (picking up her fallen books)
> Ruth! I haven't seen you…

> RUTH
> (overlapping)
> The beard looks fuller, Father. Good look for a pastor.

> FATHER DAVE
> …in church in a dog's…you think so? I was afraid I'd look like a leprechaun. I've been using this new foaming wash.

> RUTH
> (taking her books from the priest)
> Surprised the whole parish hasn't noticed. Well, I have a cake to baste, so—

FATHER DAVE

It's so good to see you, Ruth. Has Phil found work yet? This economy—I'll tell you. You think a plumber wouldn't have any...say, Ruth, why don't you come back around? Going to be an exciting year. Assumption of our Lady has a new seminarian! Young fellow. Just been assigned to us for an internship before he's—

RUTH

Okay, terrific. I have to go now, Father, before these books are late.

FATHER DAVE

Oh, right. Yes.
                (rubbing his hands together)
Yes indeed. I do hope to see more of you. Going to be an exciting year.

INT. BREW-HA-HA COFFEEHOUSE – DAY

A strip mall café. Ruth is sitting with her books and her coffee when Marcie takes a seat.

MARCIE

Did you hear about—

RUTH

No and I don't want to.

MARCIE

Suit yourself.
                (going through Ruth's books)
How ever do you find the time for all these—

RUTH

I work from home a lot. I'm allergic to cubicles and birthday clubs.

MARCIE

You given any thought to Bookends and Bookmarks? You could bring so much to our book club, Ruth. A master's in literature! The ladies would love to hear your—

                    RUTH
Bookends and Bookmarks? Is that actually the name you
settled on or was it forced upon you?

                    MARCIE
            (standing up)
Just think about it.

                    RUTH
No offense, Marcie, but *Tuesdays with Morrie* isn't exactly
my cup of tea.

                    MARCIE
You'd be surprised. We're just finishing up *Pride and
Prejudice*, and *The Crucible* is up next. Cindy's pick. It was
her turn. She doesn't like big—

                    RUTH
Cindy Drinkwater? I knew this was going to turn out to be
a coven.

                    MARCIE
Yes, Cindy. Isn't she your block captain? Just think about
it, alright? I'm late for Pilates.

                    RUTH
            (under her breath as Marcie exits)
Can't keep the Dahn Yoga Cult waiting.

INT. RUTH'S HOUSE – LIVING ROOM – DAY

Ruth enters to a seemingly empty house and puts her books down.

                    RUTH
Phil? Phil?

Danny runs in behind her shielding his bruised face.

                    RUTH (CONT'D)
Danny! Danny, where's your father? He said he was going
to fix the railing out front.

Danny shrugs as he sprints up the stairs.

> RUTH (CONT'D)

Phil! Goddammit.

Danny runs back down without his book bag and heads for the door.

> RUTH (CONT'D)

Halt!

Danny stops with his back to his mother.

> RUTH (CONT'D)

And where are you going?

> DANNY

Study group.

> RUTH

Without your books? Turn around.

Danny does so but stares at the floor. Ruth doesn't appear to notice his bruises.

> RUTH (CONT'D)
> (waving her hand)

Go, go. Just make sure you get your homework done. I don't want another phone call from Mr. Bogle.

> DANNY

Yes, Mom. Love you.

> RUTH
> (startled by the unexpected sentiment)

Right back at ya. Don't slam the—

He exits, slamming the door.

> RUTH (CONT'D)
> (yelling after him)

Say hello to the papergirl!
> (to herself, smiling a little)

Now that was just mean, Ruth.

INT. THE BLUE COMET – NIGHT

The Blue Comet Bar and Grille is a fairly dark and narrow tavern. The proprietor, NICKY, 45, sits at the far side of the bar going through receipts. His muscular physique is evident even though he is wearing a dark sharkskin suit, as he always does. What hair he has left is slicked back.

Rockabilly and Rat Pack memorabilia decorate the brick walls. The dinner specials are written on an old children's chalkboard, its edges decorated with the alphabet.

The Comet is busy tonight. The leather jacket-and-pompadour regulars lean against the bar, their bikes parked out front. Loud college kids crowd the booths while two couples, one in their twenties, the other middle-aged, enjoy dinner. Rounding out the clientele are three senior citizens, deep in their cups, planted at the bar where they are most days and nights.

Two women tend bar. Both are dressed in black with a splash of red. DARLA, 27, has a red ribbon in her dyed blond hair. Lisa Ann is dressed in tight black pants, a black shirt with three buttons undone, and a red cloth choker. FRANK, one of the three grizzled old drunks, calls Lisa Ann over and places two quarters heads up on the bar.

                    FRANK
              (slurring)
         What d'ya see, darlin'?

                    LISA ANN
         Two quarters, heads up.

                    DARLA
         Don't do it, Lisa Ann. Frank's an old hand.

                    NICKY
         Yeah, don't mess around. Just get him another whiskey
         and put him to bed.

                    FRANK
         Me, I see two pennies.

                    LISA ANN
         I bet you do.

FRANK

I see two pennies, I said. If I'm wrong, I get a buy-back.
Deal, hon?

NICKY

He's a bunko artist, Lisey. Or was.

LISA ANN
(to Frank)
Why not? You're on.

FRANK

Okay—I'm wrong.
(claps his hands once)
Tullamore Dew, neat and back, hon.

NICKY

Jesus fuck, Frank. Lisey, it's comin' outta your—

DARLA

Keep your pantaloons on, Nicky. It's only a drink.

LISA ANN

No, I'll pay. I fell and I'll pay.

NICKY

Lisey. Lisa Ann. Tell me again why you wanna go from
one building of unruly bastards to another? Being a high
school teacher ain't enough of a rush?

LISA ANN

I need the money, especially now that Paul and I—

DARLA

What you need is a man. Then you can quit this watering
hole.

NICKY

I got ears, ya know?

DARLA

Big ones at that.
(to Lisa Ann, emphatically)
A man.

             LISA ANN
        (smiling)
I got my eye on someone.

EXT. RUTH'S HOUSE – DAY (DAWN)

Casey sits on her bike with her newspaper bag slung over her shoulder. She studies the house for a moment then tosses a paper on Ruth's steps. A paperboy speeds by, shouting her name. Casey gives him the finger without turning her head and peddles away.

INT. FATHER HOSKINS HIGH – CLASSROOM #1 – DAY

Lisa Ann walks up and down the aisles collecting papers. She is wearing a dress that shows off her figure. MRS. CRITCH, the skinny, old, sour-looking algebra teacher, sticks her head in the door and curls her finger at Lisa Ann.

             MRS. CRITCH
Watch that Brendan Baar. I can't prove it, but I'm almost sure he had crib notes for my test last period.

             LISA ANN
      (in a less than serious tone)
Yes, Mrs. Critch. But crib notes for algebra? Why didn't you just go to Mr. Bogle?

             MRS. CRITCH
      (eyeing Lisa Ann's dress)
Just keep a sharp eye out. I've taught more Baars than Carter has pills.

Mrs. Critch slams the door as she leaves. Lisa Ann grins and resumes collecting papers.

             LISA ANN
Mrs. Critch just wants to keep an eye on *me*.

The class titters. BRIDGET, a heavyset girl, raises her hand. Danny watches Lisa Ann intently, and Casey watches Danny. When Lisa Ann reaches Danny's desk, she stops and casually scratches her leg, lifting her dress a little but enough for Danny to see a flash of pantyhosed thigh.

The whole show last seconds, but it catches the attention of Casey as well as Megan and Peggy. Tommy and Colin seem not to have noticed. Brendan shakes his head, as if to say "Why *him*?" Megan stage whispers, "Sleazebag" to Peggy who pleads for her friend to drop it. When Lisa Ann addresses Megan, Peggy spins around to face front. Bridget's hand is still up.

> LISA ANN
>
> Yes Megan?

> MEGAN
>
> That's a really pretty dress, Mrs. Kavanagh. Peggy was just wondering where you got it.

Peggy turns to Megan, aghast, and tries to shrink into her seat.

> LISA ANN
>
> She was, was she? Well, I'll tell you, Peggy, since your friend asked: my mother made this dress a long time ago and I'm proud to say it still fits.

> MEGAN
>
> Maybe your mom could make one for Danny's mom. He seems to——

> LISA ANN
>
> My mother's dead, Megan.

Megan deflates. Peggy hides a smile. Danny pretends to look through his book bag. Bridget uses her other hand to support her still-raised arm.

> LISA ANN (CONT'D)
>
> Jeff cap off, Casey. Pretty please. You don't want Mr. Bogle to stop by for one of his infamous spot inspections and have me hauled off to the gulag, do you?

Casey removes her jeff cap, and her cropped hair sticks up from static electricity. The students giggle, as Lisa Ann places the collected papers on her desk. The teacher risks a glance Danny's way, and he looks back. She picks up a large textbook, weighs it in her hand, and drops it into a metal wastebasket. The classroom goes silent.

> LISA ANN (CONT'D)
>
> Now that I have your attention, let's talk about ethics. Social studies class lends itself to teaching ethics, but when

we say someone is acting in an unethical manner, what are
we saying?

Bridget begins frantically waving her hand.

              MEGAN
        (as she fakes a cough into her fist)
Kiss ass.

              LISA ANN
Yes, Bridget. What are we saying when—

              BRIDGET
May I go to the lavatory please?

              LISA ANN
Of course. You should have said something.

Bridget scoots for the door clutching herself between her legs, over her
skirt. Some of the girls laugh.

              MEGAN
        (as she fakes a cough into her fist again)
Fat load.

              LISA ANN
Anyone have an answer? Well, tossing an expensive
textbook my parents paid for is pretty unethical, right, if
we define ethics as the philosophical study of morality, of
right and wrong?

Megan raises her hand.

           LISA ANN (CONT'D)
        (rubbing her temples)
Megan.

              MEGAN
You said your mom was dead.

              LISA ANN
I did. Very astute, Miss Riley, but I was being rhetorical
just now: obviously my parents didn't buy my teacher's
edition textbook. The school did.

(to the class)

So we can agree that throwing out your textbook, as fun as it may be—and it *was* very satisfying—is unethical. How about Megan's clichéd...

(as she fakes a cough into her fist)

..."loser...

(speaking)

...cough?" Ethical?

MEGAN

(without raising her hand)

I didn't do—

The bell rings. The noise level rises as the students begin gathering their books.

LISA ANN

(quietly faking a sneeze into her hands)

Spoiled brat.

MEGAN

(not sure if she heard what she thinks she did)

When I tell my mother, she'll—

LISA ANN

This cold. Can't shake it. Yes, Miss Runyon?

PEGGY

You should drink tea. My mom always makes me drink a lot of tea when I don't feel well.

The students depart. Megan, defeated again, sticks her tongue out once she is almost through the door. Danny takes his time gathering himself as does Casey. Lisa Ann rescues the textbook from the wastebasket and straightens the papers on her desk. With a sigh, Danny heads for the exit.

LISA ANN

Danny, would you mind helping me hang the new posters? I'll write you a note if I make you late for next period.

Danny nods his head, but he doesn't know where to look. Dejected, Casey slinks out. Lisa Ann hands Danny some posters, and he starts tacking up the first one.

                 LISA ANN (CONT'D)
You've done this before, I see.

                 DANNY
I have a lot of posters in my room.

Lisa Ann winces.

                 LISA ANN
Listen, Danny: Mr. Kavanagh, Paul, my husband…he,
I…we've separated. Getting a divorce actually. God—why
am I telling you this?

                 DANNY
I don't know, Mrs. Kavanagh.

                 LISA ANN
Well, no one around here knows. A divorced teacher in a
small town Catholic school isn't exactly on the tenure
track, if there was such a thing. But you know what I
mean. So let it be our little secret for now, okay? How are
you at keeping secrets, Danny?

Danny has trouble meeting her eyes. He starts to speak, hesitates, then
plunges right in.

                 DANNY
I haven't told anyone that I have a crush on you.

                 LISA ANN
                 (laughing)
Fortune favors the bold. But, good, let's keep *that* a secret
as well, although it seems some of your peers have a pretty
good idea. Best to keep them off the scent though. These
are *our* secrets.
                 (hip checking him)
I was wondering if you wanted to stay after school for a bit
today and help me out a little more. I like the way you
think, but you so rarely speak in class. I'd like to hear your
ideas out loud. How does that sound, Danny?

Danny grins and she squeezes his hand.

INT. SEVENTH HEAVEN – DAY

A loud, filthy go-go bar. Two out-of-shape dancers in pasties and g-strings gyrate lazily on a tiny stage to "Pour Some Sugar on Me" for a sparse crowd. The cocktail waitress is dressed like the dancers, and she keeps reaching around, picking and adjusting the g-string. Opposite the stage and bar is a small, sad-looking buffet. A roll is on the floor beneath the table.

In a corner booth, Phil harasses JEWELS, 29, a once-attractive but now hard-looking dancer with long black hair. She sparkles with red glitter.

> PHIL
> You did it before, Jewels. C'mon. We'll just go out to my car on your break.

He pulls a sad face. Jewels crosses her arms and legs and taps her foot.

> PHIL (CONT'D)
> You can just use your hand this time.

As she gets up to leave, he pulls her back down by her hair. She starts to scream, looking around for help, but Phil covers her mouth. He releases her hair to dig into his pants pocket, then slams his free hand on the table—his wedding ring visible—and slowly lifts it to reveal cash. Jewels settles down.

He removes his hand from her mouth and she snatches the money. His hand is covered with glitter.

> PHIL (CONT'D)
> All of it? Okay, alright. All of it then. I got it. I ain't shy about spreadin' it around—long as someone else is spreadin' too.

Jewels grabs his wrist to look at his watch then slides out of the booth.

> JEWELS
> Hand only. No touching me—and you handle cleanup. I go on break in ten. I get fifteen minutes. You'll have half that time.
> (reacting to his incredulous look)
> Hey, I gotta check on my kid and use the head. I'd go out to your car and get started if I were you.

                              PHIL
You look just like this teacher at my—

                             JEWELS
Whatever works, Phil. Parking lot in ten minutes. I'll be
whoever you want.

INT. BREW-HA-HA COFFEEHOUSE – DAY

Lisa Ann enters and sees Danny at a corner table. She looks over her
shoulder before taking a seat. An employee hangs Halloween decorations in
the front windows.

                            LISA ANN
You reserved our regular table, I see. Little early for
Halloween decorations.
              (quietly and seriously)
Danny, you haven't told anyone about our afterschool get-
togethers, right?

                            DANNY
No, Mrs. Kavanagh.

                            LISA ANN
It's not that there's anything wrong with having a chai
once in a while. It's just that it might make the other
children—students—jealous.

                            DANNY
              (when he clearly doesn't)
I understand.
              (as if to back up what he just said)
I'll be sixteen before Christmas.

                            LISA ANN
              (looking embarrassed)
I know. December 24th. A Christmas Eve baby.

                            DANNY
              (genuinely surprised)
How do you—

> LISA ANN
> Would you believe lucky guess? Maybe I could teach you
> to how to drive.

She squeezes her eyes shut briefly—*did I just say that?*—and takes Danny's
hand under the table.

EXT. BREW-HA-HA COFFEEHOUSE – DAY

Casey sits on her bicycle watching Lisa Ann and Danny from the parking
lot.

INT. BREW-HA-HA COFFEEHOUSE – DAY

The sky is a little darker. Lisa Ann takes a CD from her purse and hands it
to Danny.

> LISA ANN
> Almost forgot. He's the guy I told you about.

> DANNY
> Van the Man, right? Thank you so much.

> LISA ANN
> So…listen, Saturday? Come over my house, say around
> seven, help me hang some pictures? I'll order up a pizza.
> With Paul gone, I could use a hand. Wouldn't take long.

> DANNY
> Another secret?

She slowly brushes her hand across his cheek as she gets up to leave.

> LISA ANN
> I'll leave that decision to you. It looks like I've already
> made mine.

She leans down and whispers in his ear.

EXT. BREW-HA-HA COFFEEHOUSE – DAY

As Lisa Ann exits, she bumps into Mrs. Critch but doesn't stop or even seem to recognize her. The algebra teacher squints into the Brew-Ha-Ha and shakes her head before continuing on to another shop in the strip.

When Lisa Ann gets into her car, Casey ducks. After the teacher pulls away, the papergirl continues to watch Danny through the café's windows as he studies the CD booklet.

INT. RUTH'S HOUSE – KITCHEN – NIGHT (DUSK)

Ruth sits at the kitchen table reading *Lady Chatterley's Lover*. Danny enters through the backdoor. Ruth reluctantly puts down her book, and so begins a delicate dance between a boy with a secret and an emotionally deaf mother.

>   RUTH
>   (fighting indifference)
>   Where ya been, pal? You missed dinner—again. Don't
>   slam the—

>   DANNY
>   (as he slams the backdoor)
>   Study group.

>   RUTH
>   Right. This group must be a real hoot. Your homework
>   finished?

>   DANNY
>   (guarded)
>   Most of it. I was riding around.

>   RUTH
>   Ah, a mobile study group. You need to be careful:
>   CliffsNotes and biking is the scholastic equivalent of
>   drinking and driving. But this late hour, I half expected
>   you to come in wearing a jeff cap.
>   (when Danny doesn't respond)
>   Okay, okay. I'll stop teasing. I always hated when my
>   mother teased me about boys. It made me very shy which

in turn made me very inexperienced dating-wise when I started college.

DANNY
Is that why you married Dad? Because he was the first person who asked?

RUTH
(taken aback)
Well, that's not entirely—

DANNY
You said something like that before.

RUTH
Maybe I was angry with your dad when I said—

DANNY
When aren't you angry with him?

RUTH
Danny!

DANNY
It's okay, Mom. I'm angry with him a lot of the time too.

RUTH
You are?
(noticing him starting to shut down)
Well, love is…I sound like a greeting card from Aunt Emily, right? But love *is* complicated. Messy. Confusing. Like roller skating in the dark with knives. But apparently we can't live without it, though I'm starting to believe that I…

DANNY
That you what?

RUTH
Do you want something to eat? Do you want some tea?

Ruth gets up and puts the kettle on. After taking the saucepan from the cabinet and placing it on an unlit burner, she spoons tea leaves into a ceramic teapot.

DANNY

I'm not very hungry. Where's Dad?

RUTH

I'm usually the one asking that question. I don't know where your father is. No clue really. And I don't have to tell you that when it starts to get this late in the day and he's not here, it probably means he's not coming home till the wee hours of the morn. So it's just you and me, kiddo.
(in a Groucho voice, wiggling her
fingers)
Say the secret word, and I'll let you stay up to watch Letterman.

Danny pings the empty saucepan. Ruth smiles a little.

RUTH (CONT'D)
(singing)
"Do you hear what I hear?

Ruth looks at her son expectantly, but he doesn't bite at what must be an old family joke.

DANNY

Mom, do you think Dad's having an a—

RUTH

An affair? Well, Danny, my love, I suppose anything's possible.

DANNY

Doesn't it upset you? Make you mad?

RUTH

Upset me? Yes, but not in the way you would…I'm still here, right? Let me put it this way, sport: you know how you sprained your ankle that summer at Beach Haven? You remember how tender it was, how much it hurt, but how as time went on, even during that first week, you grew used to the way it throbbed? It didn't hurt any less probably, but what happened was your brain told your body that this was the way things were for now. So you just dealt with it. When it comes to problems that involve other people, some would call that being cold. I call it being stoic. But you say tomato and I say...

> DANNY
> (trying not to smile)
> Avocado.

Ruth reaches out to tousle his hair but stops when he flinches before she even touches him.

> RUTH
> (with a strain in her voice but diving in
> all the same)
> I ever tell you about this ceramic teapot?
> (without waiting for an answer)
> My mother made it when she was just a girl of nineteen. I guess that's still a girl. Well, my mother, she took a ceramics class at the rec center and met this guy there, one of the teachers. He took her out for tea two, three times. So she spent the better part of the remaining classes making this teapot.

While she talks, Danny takes three apples from a basket and juggles them. Ruth catches one, returning it without breaking her verbal stride. After arranging two avocados and a banana into a fruit penis, he begins fiddling with the letter magnets on the fridge. Ruth continues, forcing herself forward through Danny's antics.

> RUTH (CONT'D)
> Finally, she got up the courage to invite this man home to her mother's house for afternoon tea. He agreed, your great-grandmother was ecstatic, and my mom dolled herself up. She was so busy running around, straightening up, that when the kettle began whistling, she let it go on a bit and didn't hear the doorbell—but she thought she heard its echo. After finding no one on the porch, my mother hurried back and poured water into the teapot. She was on her way to check her hair again, when she turned around just in time to see the ceramic crack and the boiling water and tea leaves spill out.

Grinning, Danny stands back to reveal that he's spelled "balls," "ass monkey," and "boner" with the magnets. When he begins spelling a word with the letters "f" and "u," Ruth directs him away from the fridge without stopping her story. While she scatters the magnets, he puts an imaginary gun to his head, mouths "pow," and hangs his tongue out.

> RUTH (CONT'D)
> The way your grandmother told it, she just sat on the kitchen floor crying, as she tried to pick up the teapot pieces. When she realized the planned time of the ceramics teacher's arrival had passed, her crying turned to sobbing. Somehow her ears caught the sound of the bell, but when she opened the front door, there was still no one there, which set her off again.

Ruth collars Danny as he tries to sneak off.

> RUTH (CONT'D)
> Wait—here's the good part. When she returned to the kitchen to clean up, someone knocked on the backdoor, a door-to-door salesman. They had those in the dark days before the Internet. He apologized for coming to the back, but he'd been ringing the bell and when he heard sobbing, he came 'round to see what was the matter. And do you know who that man—

> DANNY
> Um, Saturday night, we have this penny poker game at Colin's. So I'm gonna stay over. Tommy too. Colin's dad taught him Texas Hold 'Em.

> RUTH
> You're supposed to rein it in on the weekends until those grades come up—and not just in social studies. Am I right? Hey, that was our deal, pal.

Danny makes a pleading face. Ruth gives in immediately.

> RUTH (CONT'D)
> Okay, okay. Who am I to stop your burgeoning gambling career? Besides, the A- in social studies *was* pretty darn impressive. But Friday, you get some homework done, kiddo. If you need pennies, there's some in—

> DANNY
> I'm alright. Going to my room now.

                              RUTH
                          (awkwardly)
                  Okey-dokey, Doggie Daddy.

Danny exits, but the tension doesn't dissipate. The kettle begins to whistle.
Ruth stares at the escaping steam.

                          RUTH (CONT'D)
                         (to herself)
          And that knight with a sample case was your grandfather,
          Danny, a man with the improbable last name of Ketel.
          Glad you never met him. Dipsomaniac. But he was a
          ceramic tile salesman when he came to the backdoor that
          portentous afternoon. A *married* ceramic tile salesman.
          Repaired this teapot, broke a marriage, and helped make
          Aunt Em and I. Therein lies the lesson: don't cry over a
          damaged pot lest you end up banging the Ketel. Or maybe
          it's: you've already broken the pot, so leave the Ketel alone
          and save yourself a fuck-load of trouble. "When the bough
          breaks / the cradle will fall / and down will come baby…"

She mouths "splat!" as she regards the back of the D. H. Lawrence book.

                          RUTH (CONT'D)
          Fuck.

Ruth goes into the other room and returns with *The Crucible*.

                          RUTH (CONT'D)
                  I must be out of my mind.

INT. THE BLUE COMET – NIGHT

It is a busy night at the Comet. Lisa Ann tends bar with Darla. Phil and
three of his cronies, STAN, BOOKER, and SHELLEY, share a booth.
Stan and Booker are around the same age as Phil. Shelley is in his late 50s.
They are obviously inebriated.

                            SHELLEY
                  It's all how you do it.

                              STAN
                  That's what I been sayin' here, Shel.

BOOKER

You ain't gonna do it, are ya, Phil? Gotta twenty says he ain't gonna do it.

PHIL

Fuck you.

SHELLEY

That's the thing. How you do it.

STAN

That's the only thing.

SHELLEY

I mean, what are we talkin' about here, Stan? We're talkin' about the thing. This thing.

BOOKER

If Philly can't pay for it, he ain't gettin' it. He's been moonin' over this skank tapstress for, what, months, right? He ain't—

PHIL

I swear, Booker…tell him, Shel. Knuckle sandwich. Without blinkin'.

STAN

Shelley knows. He's been around a time or two.

SHELLEY

Or three.

STAN

Shelley "the Sprouter" Grouter. Am I right?

SHELLEY

We're talkin' about the thing.

STAN

Or maybe it's Shelley "the Grouter" Sprouter. I always forget.

PHIL

What the fuck does that even mean, Stan? "The Grouter"?

BOOKER

I gotta twenty says you can't even get her to talk to ya. Orderin' another round don't count neither, stud. It's butterfaces or Rosie Palmer for this one. The teacher ain't givin' you a lesson, no way, no how.

STAN

"The Grouter's" the thing. Shelley knows. Tell him, Shel.

SHELLEY

I know a thing or two.

STAN

And that's the thing!

PHIL
(to Booker)
What do you know, smart ass?

BOOKER

I know you're a pussy. Go on, hit me, but it ain't gonna make it any less true. You want her, pardner? Go get her. Rope her in.

PHIL

Screw all of ya.

He turns in the booth and watches Lisa Ann. When she leaves the bar to head towards the back, Phil jumps up and accosts her in the cramped bathroom hallway.

PHIL (CONT'D)

I seen you lookin' over all night, girlie. Why didn't you come by the table, say hello? Never hurts a pretty girl to be friendly.

LISA ANN

Beat it, Phil. Get lost. I'm serious. We're busy up there. Nicky told you—

PHIL

I ain't seen Nicky around tonight. So I got an idea. Why don't you and me head out? Not now—when you get off.

He pulls a condom out of his wallet with difficulty and winks. Lisa Ann tries not to laugh.

> PHIL (CONT'D)
> Then we'll both get off. Safety's my middle name, darlin'.

> LISA ANN
> (calmly yelling)
> Nicky!

> PHIL
> Nicky's not here, babe. Now why you wanna go on denyin' what's between us, I don't know. Our spouses don't have to know a thing. 'Cept for in my car, we'll be quiet as—

> LISA ANN
> (calmly yelling again)
> Nicky!

Phil grabs her left breast and Lisa Ann knees his crotch.

> LISA ANN (CONT'D)
> (whispering in his ear as he bends over)
> Now I'm going to pretend this never happened. You're probably too hammered to notice, but it's freezing in here. Nicky's been in the cellar with the HVAC guy for hours. I don't care whether you believe me or not, but believe this: I even whisper about your little bullshit here to Nicky, your balls won't be sore anymore because they'll no longer be attached. Your new middle name will be eunuch, *darlin'*. Then you'll be real safe.

She enters the ladies' room. When a young male barback walks by, Phil straightens up, shoves the condom in his pocket, and limps back to the booth. He doesn't sit.

> STAN
> Stink finger?

> SHELLEY
> Too quick.

> PHIL
> (looking back towards the hallway)

Uppity cooze.

> BOOKER

Nice limp, Casanova. What, she kick you in the brains?

Phil punches Booker in the nose; it bleeds instantly. Stan and Shelley look elsewhere. Phil glances around, but hardly anyone in the bar seems to have noticed. He throws some napkins at Booker's bloody nose.

> PHIL

Clean yourself up, for God's sake. Somewhere else.

> BOOKER
> (as he walks away)

You know, Phil, your wife must be a real bitch.

EXT. MARCIE'S HOUSE – NIGHT

Ruth stands on the steps holding *The Crucible*.

> RUTH
> (to herself as she knocks)

I must hate myself.

INT. MARCIE'S HOUSE – LIVING ROOM – NIGHT

Marcie lets Ruth in and takes her coat. Five other women are arranged around a coffee table laden with finger foods and pastries. The women are in their sixties except for VERA, who is in her seventies, and CINDY DRINKWATER who is 49.

> MARCIE

I *never* thought you would actually show up.

> RUTH

Making casual invitations is a dangerous enterprise.

> MARCIE

Now, you know everybody.

Ruth and Cindy nod to each other.

                    MARCIE (CONT'D)
Addie Mae and Adeline are here. There's Cora and Vera
over there.

                    RUTH
Hello, hi.

                    MARCIE
Help yourself to the Brie. Cindy brought it. And we have
wine.

                    RUTH
I didn't know I was supposed to bring any—

                    MARCIE
Don't worry, honey. Have a seat. The host usually supplies
the amenities. We take turns hosting, right, ladies?

                    CINDY
But it is customary for guests to bring a *little* something.
You know the story of the perpetually empty-handed
guest.

                    RUTH
                (sitting down)
No, I missed that particular afterschool special.

A couple of the women titter. Cindy glares at them until they stop.

                    MARCIE
                (nervously to Ruth)
Oh, red or white, dear?

                    CINDY
Ruth, I haven't seen you at Mass lately.

                    RUTH
No wine for me, Marcie, thanks. I had my fill in church.
Go Assumption!

MARCIE
(sitting down)
Well, we were just getting into *The Crucible*, and Addie Mae was telling us how Marilyn Monroe converted to Judaism before she married Arthur Miller. That was her third marriage, wasn't it?

CINDY
Can we get back to the play please? *Before* we heard about Marilyn's religious flip-flopping, we were talking about the teenage whore, Abigail.

RUTH
Excuse me. I don't know the protocol here, but I always thought Abigail was both the victim and the victimizer.

CINDY
Oh, this ought to be rich.

RUTH
Yes, Abigail is the main agitator of the Salem witch hunt, and, yes, she deliberately accuses her way to John Proctor's wife. In Abigail's mind, once Elizabeth is gone, John will be free to marry her. But Proctor is thirty-five, Abby only seventeen, and he's already *known* her when she was his servant. It's not a stretch to see Abigail's behavior as a symptom of sexual abuse.

CINDY
A victim doesn't throw herself at the—

RUTH
It's traumatic bonding that comes from child grooming. Abby believes she made consensual love with John, but the truth is that she was taken, Proctor says, "where my beasts are bedded." Abigail's problem is in her head not in her vagina. John keeps playing games, telling her that he "may have looked" towards her window—wacking off most likely, not pining.

CORA
(stage whispering to Vera)
I think she means masturbation.

Cindy crosses her arms and stares at Marcie, looking vindicated.

> MARCIE
> (defensively)
> Ruth has her master's in literature.

> CINDY
> Sounds like Ruth has a master's in Masters and Johnson.

> RUTH
> There's even an argument to be made that Proctor is both victim and victimizer as well. Though they usually married when they were in their twenties, there wasn't an age of consent in the Puritan community. In other words, if there's grass on the infield, play ball. Proctor only fouls out by committing adultery.

> MARCIE
> (wanting this to end)
> Pizzelle anyone? Made them this morning.

> RUTH
> To try to stem the tide of the witch hunts, he confesses about Abigail in court. In order to save his name, he refuses to lie, to name names, after he's been arrested and so goes to the gallows seemingly absolved.

> CINDY
> Oh, so now you like him? The rapist is the hero?

Ruth gives a little smile. Cora and Vera clutch each other. Marcie rubs her forehead.

> RUTH
> I never used the word rape. My point was: is anybody all good or all bad?

> CINDY
> We know who the villain is from the first few pages. Abigail tries—

> RUTH
> Her world comes crashing down when Proctor tells her, "We never touched, Abby." You remember your first time,

how you felt. Now imagine that the person you gave it to—or who stole it, rather—denies it ever happened.

CORA
(stage whispering to Vera)
I think she means defloration.

ADDIE MAE
My first kiss was from Edgar, and I married him.

CINDY
If the play is this obscene, it should be banned from our schools. Sex may impress you, Ruth, but I can say it never made me do anything crazy...

RUTH
(overlapping)
Then you're not doing it right.

CINDY
...and I think talking about it serves no purpose but to stir—

RUTH
(getting up)
Stir the devil. Yes, I've heard that speech from you before, and I can honestly believe that you've never stirred anyone. Next time you go south on Hank, Cindy, have him drink pineapple juice first. His stuff'll go down easier. Maybe then he'll be able to lose those hangdog eyes.

CORA
(stage whispering to Vera)
I think she means fellatio.

VERA
A blowjob. I know. I wasn't born old. I used to be quite good at them.

CINDY
I didn't see Phil at any of Danny's games last summer. Happy hour start early at McCullough's or the Blue Comet?

>   MARCIE
> Okay, ladies, ladies.

She retrieves Ruth's coat and walks her outside.

EXT. MARCIE'S HOUSE – NIGHT

>   MARCIE
> I thought Bookends and Bookmarks was more your speed,
> but maybe the Queenie Quilt Club—

>   RUTH
> You need to work on those coven names, Marcie.
> Goodnight.

>   MARCIE
> See you in church?

>   RUTH
> You betcha. But all this stirring of the devil: I just hope the
> holy water doesn't hiss when I put my fingers in the font.

As Marcie opens the door to return:

>   CINDY
> The only husband *she* should be worried about is her own.
> Phil's the only plumber I know whose snake is more than
> just an electric eel.

Ruth wears a tight smile as the door shuts.

EXT. THE BLUE COMET – NIGHT

Phil, Stan, and Shelley, all quite drunk, stand in an alley across the street
from the bar.

>   STAN
> Booker's just mad is all. I mean, he didn't have a nice nose
> before but—

The bar signs go out.

> PHIL

Shhh.

> SHELLEY

This is definitely not the thing.

> STAN

Shel would know, Phil. Shel knows about a whole hell of a lot of things. Some of them even useful.

> PHIL

Zip it. Here they come.

The male cook exits the bar followed by two young waitresses chattering with the barback. Darla and Lisa Ann exit next. The women hug. Darla walks down the street, and Lisa Ann crosses over towards the alley.

> SHELLEY

They didn't lock it, Phil.

> PHIL

You want me to break your shnozz too?

> SHELLEY

Here's the thing: they didn't lock the door.

As Lisa Ann passes the alley, Phil jumps out and grabs her, putting one of her arms behind her back.

> PHIL

You don't know a good thing when it's swingin' right in front of your pretty brown eyes, sister.

> LISA ANN

Phil? Phil, let me go. For God's sake, I teach your—

> PHIL

You don't mess with a man's jewels, baby. Don't you know that?

Large arms encircle Phil's neck and chest, lifting him off the ground and forcing him to release Lisa Ann. When he's dropped, Phil turns just in time to receive a haymaker from Nicky. Stan and Shelley run down the alley.

Nicky leans down to fix his hair in the reflection of a car window. Lisa Ann collects herself as Darla runs over.

> NICKY
>
> You alright, Lisey?

> LISA ANN
>
> I'm okay. Thanks. I think he's out cold.

> NICKY
>
> Warm, cold. He's out. Listen, you girls walk out with me from now on, and if I ain't here, I'll tell Bobby or Carlo to walk you to your cars.

> DARLA
>
> Should we call his wife?

> NICKY
>
> Not unless you wanna deal with that headache. Naw, I say let him stew in his own juices a while. It's a small town. He'll still have his pants on when he wakes up. C'mon, lemme take you to your cars before I get it in my head to depants him myself.

INT. RUTH'S HOUSE – UPSTAIRS BATHROOM – NIGHT (DUSK)

In the mirror, Danny checks his hair and touches the light peach fuzz on his upper lip.

> DANNY
> (to himself)
> You're not a little boy anymore.

INT. RUTH'S HOUSE – LIVING ROOM – NIGHT (DUSK)

Ruth is reading *The Bell* by Iris Murdoch and drinking tea. Danny runs down the stairs.

> RUTH
>
> Halt. Destination please.

> DANNY
> I told you. Sleeping over Tommy's for the poker thingie.

> RUTH
> Your homework finished?

> DANNY
> Most of it. But, Mom, it's Saturday.

> RUTH
> Well, just make sure you finish it tomorrow.

> DANNY
> Fine.

> RUTH
> And don't tell your father.

He gives her an incredulous look, and she waves him off.

> RUTH (CONT'D)
> Right. Go forth and be brave.

Danny exits.

> RUTH (CONT'D)
> (yelling after him)
> No kiss goodbye anymore?
> (to herself)
> "Don't tell your father." Good one, Ruth. He'd have to go to Mustang Sally's Stopless Go-Go or maybe Bottoms Up to tell his father anything.

Humming "Mustang Sally," Ruth tosses *The Bell* aside and picks up *Idylls of the King* by Alfred Lord Tennyson.

INT. LISA ANN'S HOUSE – LIVING ROOM – NIGHT

Lisa Ann is on the phone with Paul. While they speak, she sits on the edge of the sofa, paging through a Father Hoskins High School Yearbook.

> PAUL (V.O.)
> I'll pick up the last of it next week.

LISA ANN

That's fine. No hurry.
> (beat)

Paul?

PAUL (V.O.)

What is it?

LISA ANN

When we got together back at the university, when we got married, I know your mother had a hard time with it. The age difference and all.

She stops paging through the yearbook and runs her finger down a recent photo of Danny.

PAUL (V.O.)
> (chuckling)

I'll say she did. She didn't speak to me for two whole weeks, which in mother time is like seventy—

LISA ANN

But did you?

PAUL (V.O.)

Did I what?

LISA ANN

Did you struggle with it at all? You know: oh shit, the girl I'm marrying still has the scent of Barbies on her. What does she know about life? I mean, there *was* a significant age difference, Paul.

PAUL (V.O.)

Still is. A twenty year age difference but fourteen great years together. And there's no way you ever had a Barbie doll.

LISA ANN

Yeah.

When she turns the page there is a picture of Danny at the Freshman Dance. He looks incredibly young, and she slams the book shut.

PAUL (V.O.)
Okay, so maybe not all of them were great, but we always got along. We always had that.

LISA ANN
But it wasn't enough, was it?

PAUL (V.O.)
I guess not for you. But why the questions?

Lisa Ann looks out her windows and sees Danny approaching on his bike. She stashes the yearbook between the sofa cushions.

LISA ANN
No reason. Just asking.

PAUL (V.O.)
You always end up telling me, so just spill the beans.

LISA ANN
I'll tell you later. Maybe. I have to go.

INT. RUTH'S HOUSE – LIVING ROOM – NIGHT

Phil, his face swollen and bruised, looks for his keys. Ruth has a finger in her book.

RUTH
So your face bruised itself during your sleepover? No? How odd. And you're so well liked and admired. Well, thanks for the drive-by. Always happy to contribute to a stripper's college fund. Don't slam—

Phil exits, slamming the door. Ruth raises her hand to throw the book but thinks better of it.

RUTH (CONT'D)
Someone ought to throw the book at you, Phil, and not just at your face.

INT. LISA ANN'S HOUSE – DINING ROOM – NIGHT

"Into the Mystic" from *Moondance* plays on the stereo. Danny stands on a stepladder, hammering a nail through a picture hanger. Lisa Ann supports him with one hand on his stomach, the other on his hip. Danny looks down. It's obvious he has an erection. Embarrassed, he descends the ladder and holds the framed picture in front of his waist.

                    DANNY
          I'm sorry, Mrs. Kavanagh.

Lisa Ann takes the picture from Danny's hands and leans it against the wall.

                    LISA ANN
          I told you: here, I'm Lisa Ann. So repeat after me: Lisa
          Ann.

                    DANNY
          Lisa Ann. And I'm still sorry.

                    LISA ANN
          I'm not. Why be? It's natural. At home, don't you take
          matters into your own…never mind.

                    DANNY
          It hurts a little. I think I should probably go. I want to stay,
          but I—

                    LISA ANN
               (caressing his face)
          Do you want me to make it stop hurting?

                    DANNY
               (short of breath)
          What kind of secret would that be?

                    LISA ANN
               (looking down)
          Not a little one.

EXT. LISA ANN'S HOUSE – NIGHT

All the lights are out. Paul gets out of his car and knocks on the backdoor, shouting.

> PAUL
> Lisa Ann? I see your car. Are you home? Lisa Ann? I just didn't think you sounded so good on the phone.

He regards the backdoor handle, but shakes his head and doesn't try it. Turning to leave, he notices Danny's bike leaning against the wall and gently kicks the front tire before departing.

INT. PHIL'S CAR – NIGHT

Parked outside of Lisa Ann's house, Phil finishes off a bottle of cheap whiskey and throws it in the backseat as he watches Paul drive away. The car's clock reads 9:34 p.m. He tries to open another bottle but discovers that he is unable to keep his eyes open. He falls asleep…

INT./EXT. PHIL'S CAR – NIGHT (LATER)

…and when he wakes, it is near midnight according to the car's clock. In a foggy kind of panic, he falls out of the vehicle when he opens the door and eventually weaves his way to Lisa Ann's low fence and tumbles over it.

INT. MARCIE'S HOUSE – BEDROOM – NIGHT

Marcie watches Phil through her binoculars while she talks on the phone.

> CINDY (V.O.)
> First one, now the other?

> MARCIE
> But that's not all. Someone's in there with her.

She is instantly sorry that she said anything.

> HAROLD
> (in bed)
> I wonder if it's quieter over there.

> CINDY (V.O.)

Who?

A fearful look comes over Marcie's face as she moves the focus of her binoculars from Lisa Ann's dining room windows to the bicycle, visible in the porch light, and back to the windows again,. Candles flicker within. Marcie watches a shadow on the wall become two shadows that quickly merge again.

> CINDY (V.O. CONT'D)

Marcie? Who?

> MARCIE
> (obviously lying)

I don't know. No one. Maybe she's not even home. It's late. I have to go to bed. Early Mass tomorrow.

> CINDY (V.O.)
> (as Marcie is hanging up)

Marcie? Who's in there? Who does the hussy have—

EXT. LISA ANN'S HOUSE – NIGHT

As Phil creeps up to the dining room windows, the shadows part again. One disappears briefly, then returns. More candles are lit.

When he reaches the windows, he watches Lisa Ann and Danny, both naked, feed each other cake. In the background, "Baby, Please Don't Go" by Them finishes up in a hot hurray. It's followed by the piano and strings opening of Van Morrison's "Have I Told You Lately." Phil clutches his chest, staggers back to his car, and speeds away.

INT. RUTH'S HOUSE – LIVING ROOM – NIGHT

Phil storms into the house. Ruth, who fell asleep reading on the sofa, is startled awake.

> RUTH

Danny? That you, kiddo? Get wiped out early in the big tourney?

> (realizing who just came in)
> Phil? What, run out of dollar bills to stick in Sapphire or
> Bambi's g-string?

Phil ignores her and heads up the stairs.

INT. RUTH'S HOUSE – MASTER BEDROOM – NIGHT

Phil opens the closet and retrieves a gun hidden in a cowboy boot.

INT. RUTH'S HOUSE – KITCHEN – NIGHT

Ruth lights the burner beneath the tea kettle. The saucepan is next to it. Phil
enters and takes a bottle of whiskey from a cabinet. Ruth stares at the
knight on the cover of *Idylls of the King* and shakes her head.

RUTH

> Don't you think you've had—

Phil seizes the ceramic teapot and throws it to the floor before exiting via
the backdoor.

EXT. RUTH'S HOUSE – NIGHT

Phil pauses in the driveway. pulls the gun from the back of his pants, and
checks the barrel.

INT. RUTH'S HOUSE – KITCHEN – NIGHT

Ruth stares at the ceramic shards before picking them up and tossing them
in the trashcan, all while talking to herself.

RUTH

> Oh, Mom, unless my Lancelot falls from Heaven, I think
> I'm shit out of luck. Then again, I don't think you
> envisioned a life where you were always trying to fix what
> was broken. Your door-to-door salesman sold you a bill of
> goods: yeah, Dad could fix a teapot, but everything else he
> fucked up or just fucked.

EXT. LISA ANN'S HOUSE – DAY (DAWN)

Her newspaper bag slung over her shoulder, Casey sits on her bicycle and stares at Danny's bike, still on Lisa Ann's back porch. After looking around, she leaves her paper bag with her bike and quietly makes her way to the backdoor. Finding it unlocked. Casey eases the door open and enters the house.

INT. PHIL'S CAR – DAY (DAWN)

Phil is passed out with the gun in his hand. He is covered in red glitter.

INT. MARCIE'S HOUSE – KITCHEN – DAY (DAWN)

Over coffee, Marcie uses her binoculars to watch Casey pause at a second floor window in Lisa Ann's house.

INT. LISA ANN'S HOUSE – UPSTAIRS HALLWAY – DAY (DAWN)

Casey peaks into the master bedroom and sees two pairs of feet entangled in the bedding.

EXT. LISA ANN'S HOUSE – DAY (DAWN)

Casey comes tearing out of the house.

INT. MARCIE'S HOUSE – KITCHEN – DAY (DAWN)

Marcie watches Casey take off, skid to a stop, and circle back for her paper bag. The girl never takes her eyes off Lisa Ann's house. Marcie trains her binoculars on Phil's car, frowns, and moves to the back porch to focus on Danny's bike: *it's still there.*

INT. PHIL'S CAR – DAY

Phil wakes with a start and struggles to read the clock: 8:45 a.m. Looking confused…

EXT. LISA ANN'S HOUSE – DAY

…he leaps out of the car, hops the fence, and peaks into the dining room windows.

> PHIL
> (to himself)
> No kid, no candles, no cake, not even crumbs. What the fuck was I smoking?

He hurries to his car, pausing only to throw up in a cloud of red glitter.

INT. PHIL'S CAR – DAY

Phil pulls out on Highland Avenue. In his rearview mirror, he watches a police patrol car pull up in front of Lisa Ann's house, and he blows a red light.

INT. MARCIE'S HOUSE – KITCHEN – DAY

> MARCIE
> The police are here, Harold. It's about time too. It's only been how many hours since I called?
> (squinting at the clock: 11:05 a.m.)
> He's been in that house all night. God knows what they're—

INT. LISA ANN'S HOUSE – UPSTAIRS HALLWAY – DAY

Lisa Ann and Danny stand facing each other without much space between them. Both look hastily dressed. She briefly attempts to tame his bedhead as she speaks. Danny cannot stop touching the teacher: her arm, her covered breast, her hair.

> LISA ANN
> You have to go now. There's no time. I'll be fine. Out the back. Go! Now!

EXT. LISA ANN'S HOUSE – DAY

The backdoor slams. Danny grabs his bike and leaves through a side gate.

INT. BLACK SEDAN – DAY

> DETECTIVE COTTEN
> (on the radio)
> Pick her up. Let me know when it's done.
> (to himself)
> There's gonna be a feeding frenzy once they book her.

INT. MARCIE'S HOUSE – LIVING ROOM – DAY

While on the phone, Marcie watches Lisa Ann's house through her binoculars.

> MARCIE
> They're bringing her out.

> CINDY (V.O.)
> Let's see how Ruth St. Clair feels about John Proctor now.

EXT. LISA ANN'S HOUSE – DAY

Lisa Ann, wearing a blank expression, is led out of her house in handcuffs. There are two police cars out front now, silently flashing their lights. A uniformed officer puts Lisa Ann in one of the patrol cars. The teacher squeezes her eyes shut then opens them.

INT. CASEY'S HOUSE – LIVING ROOM – DAY

Casey sits between her parents as she speaks to two plainclothes detectives, Cotten and WELLES. The girl appears to be cycling through a range of emotions. CASEY'S MOTHER takes her daughter's jeff cap off and puts it on an end table.

> DETECTIVE COTTEN
> You did the right thing, Casey, having your parents call us

when they did. And we thank you for letting us come back here today to talk with you again. Now there's probably gonna be even more questions in the future from people other than us, but they all want to make sure the right thing is done here and they all want to protect you. I know it's gonna be hard to do, but you need to stop worrying. We're gonna take care of it. You don't want to end up like my partner Welles here. His forehead looks like a wrinkled carpet in a bad restaurant. You go on back to being you.

Cotten stands and picks up the cap. After looking at it for a moment, he places it back on Casey's head.

EXT. CASEY'S HOUSE – DAY

Cotten takes a pinky ball from his jacket pocket. During the detectives' conversation, Cotten throws the ball against the stoop and attempts to catch it. It's obviously a familiar habit.

> DETECTIVE WELLES
> The old lady with the binoculars? She says a couple of minutes after the first patrol car pulled up to Kavanagh's place, the kid barrels outta the backdoor, hops on his bike, and hightails it down Renfrew Road. By the time she told the officers, the kid was long gone. She ID'd him though.

> DETECTIVE COTTEN
> Danny St. Clair.

> DETECTIVE WELLES
> She said he was there all night. In a way, she's a better witness than—

> DETECTIVE COTTEN
> The papergirl? They're gonna call it criminal trespass, but I believe Casey thought something was wrong and went in to check it out.

He grunts as the ball almost flies over his head.

> DETECTIVE COTTEN (CONT'D)
> When Kavanagh spoke to the arresting officers, she told them *twice* that she and the kid were in love—not exactly

confessions, but they're good starts. The officers said it sounded like she was sobbing but her eyes and face were dry. That's why I want to get as much sewn up today as we can. I don't want what happened in Bucks County, where the teacher walked 'cause of bad police work, to happen here. When the algebra teacher called this morning, it was like it was being handed to us, which is why I want the arrest to be ironclad. It's starting to seem too easy, minus the missing kid.

The ball bounces off the stoop and narrowly misses Welles' head. Cotten catches the pinky as it rebounds off a parked car. Welles sighs.

> DETECTIVE COTTEN (CONT'D)
> Helps me focus my thinking.

The next ball hits Welles' forehead.

> DETECTIVE WELLES
> So you always tell me.

> DETECTIVE COTTEN
> We need that search warrant. Let's play it safe.

> DETECTIVE WELLES
> She could have washed the sheets already.

> DETECTIVE COTTEN
> Doubt it. From what the officers told me, it's more likely that she laminated them. But her proclamations of love, along with her possible lamentation put-ons, tell me that dollars to donuts, she doesn't really know why she did it. You don't boldly declare love as your possible defense, then fake cry. Who was that little show for? The arresting officers? No, it was for her. She's trying on different reactions to find the right one.

Cotten chases the pinky ball into the street, where it bounces off a passing car. Cotten lunges to catch it and returns grinning.

> DETECTIVE WELLES
> So with the old ladies' statements…

                    DETECTIVE COTTEN
          (overlapping)
     Dietlin and Critch.

                    DETECTIVE WELLES
     …on top of the girl's in there, don't we have enough for
     the Chief to—

                    DETECTIVE COTTEN
     Kick it up to the DA's office? Yes indeed. "A" for effort,
     Welles. Go kick-start those warrants, yeah? Don't worry:
     she's not gonna lawyer up, not yet. We'll interview her
     tonight.

                    DETECTIVE WELLES
          (ducking the pinky ball)
     And the kid?

                    DETECTIVE COTTEN
     Something tells me Danny's gonna return home on his
     own, if we don't find him first. Regardless, I'm gonna have
     to talk to his parents once the social worker from Child
     Services gets here.

                    DETECTIVE WELLES
     It's time for the teacher to get detention.

Cotten doesn't even try to catch the pinky.

                    DETECTIVE COTTEN
     Really, Welles? You have to work on your—

INT. RUTH'S HOUSE – LIVING ROOM – NIGHT (DUSK)

The tea kettle is whistling. Someone knocks on the door. Ruth hurries
down the stairs, straightens the family picture, and heads for the kitchen.

                    RUTH
     Phil! Phil, can you get the door? Danny! Danny, can you
     answer the—

The doorbell rings. More knocking.

                    RUTH (CONT'D)
Coming!
          (to herself as she walks to the door)
Please be an eager Girl Scout hawking Thin Mints out of
season. I already have this month's *Watchtower*.

She stops briefly to look into the entranceway mirror. When she opens the
door, a Halloween skeleton decoration falls off. A uniformed Mondauk
Proper police officer stands on the steps just behind Carol and Detective
Cotten, who takes out his badge.

                    RUTH (CONT'D)
I knew it was a little early for trick or treating. Jesus. What
did my husband do now? He actually pee *on* a stripper this
time rather than—

                 DETECTIVE COTTEN
Ruth St. Clair?

                      CAROL
          (urgently)
We need to talk to you and your husband. It's about your
son. It's about Danny.

The kettle continues to whistle.

INT. RUTH'S HOUSE – KITCHEN – NIGHT (DUSK)

Phil quietly enters through the backdoor. There is still red glitter on his face
and clothes. He can hear Ruth speaking with Cotten and Carol in the living
room. He breathes into his hand.

INT. RUTH'S HOUSE – BASEMENT – NIGHT (DUSK)

Phil descends the basement stairs and sticks the gun in a dusty toolbox. In a
tiny bathroom, he washes his face and attempts to brush the glitter off his
clothes. He pulls his pants down and stands on his toes to wash his
privates, sprinkling the sink with more red glitter.

                    RUTH (O.S.)
Phil? Is that you? Are you down there?

Phil inspects his face in the mirror as he continues to soap his genitalia. He realizes he is becoming aroused and pulls the door closed.

> PHIL
> (breathing heavily)
> I'll be up in a sec.

EXT. RUTH'S STREET – NIGHT (DUSK)

The last of the light is leaving the day. Danny skids to a stop on his bicycle at the top of the block when he sees the police car and the black sedan blocking the driveway. After a moment, he starts to cry and slowly pedals home.

INT. RUTH'S HOUSE – LIVING ROOM – NIGHT

Phil enters and stands near but not next to his wife. He brushes away some glitter from his shirt but notices Cotten watching him and stops.

> RUTH
> But I don't understand. His social studies teacher? I thought Mr. Peitzman was his—

> DETECTIVE COTTEN
> Lisa Ann Kavanagh. *Mrs.* Lisa Ann Kavanagh, but it appears she's separated from her husband. Divorce in the works. Let's see: thirty-four-years-old. She's been teaching at Father Hoskins High since—

> RUTH
> How old? I don't understand. She did what now?

> DETECTIVE COTTEN
> The illicit "relationship" began around the start of the school year. What we don't know yet is when it—

Phil begins to shake.

> RUTH
> Phil, say something, say—

PHIL

She's getting divorced? The bitch is getting *divorced?*

RUTH

Wait—do you know this woman, Phil? Do you know—

PHIL

That wasn't no dream, the cake and all. Jesus fucking Christ. She's finally dumping the old man, and she chose *him?* She chose *my kid?*

INT. RUTH'S HOUSE – KITCHEN – NIGHT

Danny enters through the backdoor, wipes his face on his sleeve, and takes a deep breath.

INT. RUTH'S HOUSE – LIVING ROOM – NIGHT

Danny walks into the living room. After a few silent seconds, Phil attacks his son, slapping his face and squeezing his neck. He is quickly subdued and handcuffed, but not before Ruth punches his bruised face, drawing blood. The uniformed officer speaks into his radio. Another cop enters and escorts Phil out.

Ruth rushes to her son but stops just short.

RUTH

Danny? Are you okay? Danny? What did she…?

DETECTIVE COTTEN

Danny, would you like us to take you to the ER?

Danny straightens his shirt and shakes his head. Cotten nods in assent.

CAROL

This is domestic violence, detective. Under the circumstances I think we should—

DETECTIVE COTTEN

I wouldn't. Just keep an eye. The ER can be a circus. We gotta take him to Holy Redeemer later anyway.

(to Danny)

Just for a quick exam, Danny. In and out.

(under his breath to Carol)

Let the kid feel like he's in control of something. His father's a lush and the least of our problems. We can revisit what just happened later if necessary.

CAROL

Okay, fine, yeah.

(to Danny)

Something to drink maybe, Danny? No? Well, my name is Carol, and I'm a social worker with Child Welfare Services.

She extends her hand, but Danny just stares at the floor.

DETECTIVE COTTEN

And I'm Detective Joe Cotten with the Special Victims Unit. Why don't you and your mom sit down, take a load off?

He directs them to a love seat. Mother and son sit as far apart as they can. They both look embarrassed. Danny studies his sneakers.

RUTH

I have to tell you, I don't know what I should be feeling here.

CAROL

A period of emotional adjustment is natural and normal for the entire family in a time such as this, Mrs. St. Clair. Now, Danny, just tell us what happened in your own words. Take your time. We don't have to finish tonight, but it's more comfortable here, so we might as well start.

The detective flips open a notebook. Carol takes out a small tape recorder but before placing it on the coffee table, she looks at Ruth, who nods.

RUTH

Danny, just...

DETECTIVE COTTEN

(patting Danny's knee)

You can do it, son.

Danny doesn't lift his head.

> CAROL
> (to Ruth)
> Maybe if you…maybe if we speak with Danny alone, we could—

> RUTH
> (nervously standing)
> Certainly, if…Danny, do you want me to leave the room?
> (to Carol and Cotten)
> Are you talking about taking him to the station or…?

> DETECTIVE COTTEN
> This is fine for now.

There is a moment of silence after which the detective closes his notebook.

> DETECTIVE COTTEN (CONT'D)
> Listen, son: we spoke with Mrs. Kavanagh. She's in custody now. She told us about you and her. We just want to hear it from you. You're not in any trouble. None at all.

Ruth sits down again.

> CAROL
> You didn't do anything wrong. Your teacher acted inappropriately.

> DETECTIVE COTTEN
> Say something, son. Anything.

> CAROL
> We're just here for you, to look out for your well-being.

She glances at Ruth who lowers her eyes.

> DANNY
> (to Ruth)
> Can I go to my room now?

> RUTH
> (looking up after a beat)
> No. You may not.

The detective and the social worker make eye contact.

                    CAROL
Excuse us for a moment.

Cotten and Carol move to the front door and speak in low voices.

               DETECTIVE COTTEN
He's embarrassed to talk about it in front of his mother.

                    CAROL
But won't it rattle him more if we take him to the station?
You didn't even want to go to the ER.

               DETECTIVE COTTEN
Different Garanimals. Station might rattle him enough to
talk. Besides, home, sweet, home smells a little rank.

                    CAROL
Okay, fine, yeah. But if he gets worse, starts blaming
himself—

               DETECTIVE COTTEN
There's a shrink on site. But if he still remains silent? We'll
go to plan C.

                    CAROL
Which is?

               DETECTIVE COTTEN
I don't know. One letter at a time.

EXT. RUTH'S HOUSE – NIGHT

Cotten helps Danny into the back of the black sedan. Carol is in the
passenger seat. She turns to smile at Danny, but he just stares out the
window as Ruth stumbles to her car.

INT. POLICE STATION – NIGHT

A POLICEMAN escorts Phil to GREGGS, the desk officer, to sign for his
personal effects. Greggs is older than the other cop.

POLICEMAN

You're lucky, pal. We could have arrested you on any number of charges, so why don't you just sober up and take care of your kid. He needs his...

PHIL
(overlapping, muttering as he exits)
Shove it up your ass.

POLICEMAN

...father now. What did you say?

GREGGS

He told you to pucker up and like it.

POLICEMAN

Jag-off. His kid just got molested, and he's acting like—

GREGGS

I seen her. His kid got an education far as I can tell. Lucky bastard.

POLICEMAN

There's something wrong with you, Greggs.

GREGGS

Hey, I woulda killed for that kinda action when I was a kid. But no one even gave me a ball squeeze. Not even our priest.

The policeman walks away in disgust.

EXT. POLICE STATION – NIGHT

Phil gets into a cab that departs just as Ruth and company arrive.

INT. POLICE STATION – NIGHT

Ruth and Danny follow Cotten and Carol down a hallway of closed doors.

>   DANNY
>   (to Ruth, pointing to the doors)
>   She's behind one of those, isn't she?

Ruth doesn't answer.

>   DANNY (CONT'D)
>   Please let me see her. Just let me talk to her.
>   (taking hold of Ruth's sleeve)
>   We love each other, Mom. She's my brown eyed girl.

Ruth stops walking.

>   DANNY (CONT'D)
>   Don't do to me what you've done to Dad.

Ruth starts to reply but holds her tongue. Danny gestures to Cotten, who leans down so the boy can whisper in his ear.

>   DETECTIVE COTTEN
>   Mrs. St. Clair, Danny would feel more comfortable if he
>   spoke with us alone. Are you okay with—

Ruth nods, staring at her son as if seeing him for the first time.

>   RUTH
>   I'll be…here.

Ruth walks away as Cotten leads Danny into a free room. She sings under her breath like she is trying to remember something.

>   RUTH (CONT'D)
>   "Laughin' and a-runnin', hey hey / skippin' and a jumpin' /
>   In the misty mornin' fog / with our hearts a thumpin'/
>   and you…"

She stops and turns to look up the hallway.

>   RUTH (CONT'D)
>   "…my brown eyed girl…"
>   (out loud to no one)
>   He's not a baby. He's not.

INT. RUTH'S HOUSE – BASEMENT – NIGHT

Phil removes the gun from the toolbox, admires it, and sticks it in the back of his pants.

EXT. POLICE STATION – NIGHT

Ruth and Danny leave the police station.

INT. RUTH'S CAR – NIGHT

Danny gets into the back seat. Ruth pauses before pulling out of the lot.

> RUTH
> God, it's cold out tonight.
> > (beat)
> Carol was a nice woman, huh? A little abrupt maybe, but...
> > (turning the radio on)
> This okay? God, it's cold. Bet you can't wait for baseball season to start.
> > (beat)
> You don't need to worry about your father. Once he sobers up...

She stops talking and concentrates on driving.

INT. RUTH'S CAR – NIGHT (LATER)

Ruth pulls into the driveway. She adjusts the rearview mirror to better see her son.

> RUTH
> Listen, Danny—

> DANNY
> > (calmly and coldly)
> I will never talk to you again.

He gets out of the car. Ruth moves the mirror so she can watch herself break down.

INT. RUTH'S HOUSE – UPSTAIRS HALLWAY – NIGHT

Ruth stands outside of Danny's bedroom staring at the Flyers and Phillies pictures, cut from sports magazines, that are taped to his door.

She jumps when "Mannish Boy," the live version from the *Last Waltz* album, blares from Danny's speakers: "Now when I was a young boy at the age of five / My mother said I was gonna be the greatest man alive." Ruth slowly backs away. "But now I'm a man, way past twenty-one / I want you to believe me, woman, I had lots of fun."

INT. RUTH'S HOUSE – UPSTAIRS BATHROOM – NIGHT

Ruth finishes brushing her teeth and stares into the mirror. As she speaks to herself, she violently rips out grey hairs until her scalp bleeds.

> RUTH
> If a girl is assaulted, they say she must have welcomed it somehow, so she goes from being one kind of victim to another: a presumed victim of her own desires. Happens more often than you think, kiddo. Then there's your father, always the victim even though nothing ever happens to him. His mother smacked his ass once or twice and the rest of us suffer.

Ruth takes some mouthwash, as Van Morrison and the Band get to the heart of "Caravan" in Danny's room: "Switch on your electric light / Then we can get down to what's really wrong, really wrong, really wrong…" Ruth spits the mouthwash on the mirror and studies her distorted face behind the dripping blue liquid.

> RUTH (CONT'D)
> I'll never let them make you a victim. I'll never make you feel like you did something bad, not if I can help it. I can do that much.

INT. MONDAUK COUNTY CORRECTIONAL FACILITY – DAY

Lisa Ann, in the standard blue MCCF attire, sits across the table from NORMAN FAIRLIE, a mild-looking attorney.

NORMAN

Mrs. Kavanagh, I'm Norman Fairlie from the firm of
Kasstner and Felt. To get any, uh, unpleasantness out of
the way, your husband—

LISA ANN

Ex.

NORMAN

Yes, well, uh, separated. When your…when Mr. Kavanagh
retained me, he said he would take care of, uh, all—

LISA ANN
(lowering her head a moment)
I understand.

NORMAN

Fine, fine. So, uh, first we need to appeal your bail denial.
It was predicated upon your repeated affirmations of, uh,
romantic love for the St. Clair boy.

LISA ANN

Danny. His name is Danny. And we don't need to appeal
anything. I'm right where I belong.

NORMAN

I see. Well, our investigator has been busy since Mr.
Kavanagh contacted the firm, and we, uh, are armed with
information we wouldn't normally have at this juncture.
Now, the crucial issue is reaching a plea agreement, which
will take time to hammer out, but—

LISA ANN

I don't want a plea agreement either.

NORMAN

Yes, well, perhaps you should speak with Mr. Kavanagh.

LISA ANN

Paul is very good to me. I don't want to waste his money.
Go on, please.

NORMAN

The DA's office is pursuing a number of felony charges.

The ADA has been adamant that there would be no plea agreement, but he, uh, appears to be changing his tune, so to speak. We suspect a variety of reasons. Much of the county's case hinges on the testimony of Miss Casey Grace, but her eyewitness account was, uh, in my opinion, obtained through illegal means, and the ADA knows it. Another important witness, Mrs. Marcille Dietlin, turns out to be in the intermediate stage of macular degeneration, so we could contest her—

                    LISA ANN
That's awful. I've known Marcie Dietlin for years.

                    NORMAN
Yes, yes. Well, witnesses aside, there's the matter of the disjointed statements you gave during questioning, which they are treating as a confession. But you didn't sign anything, and while you didn't deny their accusations, you didn't, uh, admit guilt. We could state that anything you said was obtained while you were under duress.

Lisa Ann shakes her head.

                    NORMAN (CONT'D)
No. Fine, fine. But we might not need to worry about your statements or even the witnesses. Fortune, uh, favors the lucky.

                    LISA ANN
How's that?

                    NORMAN
It doesn't appear the boy—Danny—is going to cooperate. At all. Of course, that doesn't mean he won't before this case is resolved, but, uh, for now—

                    LISA ANN
                    (distressed)
Tell him he *must*.

                    NORMAN
                    (confused)
Tell who?

> LISA ANN
> Danny. Tell Danny he has to answer all their questions. He has to talk.

> NORMAN
> (flummoxed)
> Why would—

> LISA ANN
> It wasn't real if he doesn't. It wouldn't be real then.

INT. RUTH'S HOUSE – UPSTAIRS HALLWAY – DAY

Danny, fully dressed with his book bag over his shoulder, passes Ruth in the hall.

> RUTH
> Where are you going?

Without looking back, Danny points to his book bag.

> RUTH (CONT'D)
> School? It's only been a week and half. They said you could take as long as you needed. Are you sure?

Danny continues down the stairs without answering. Ruth leans on the railing and sips her tea from a Best Mom Ever mug.

INT. RUTH'S HOUSE – KITCHEN – DAY

Danny enters. His father, looking especially flushed and bloated in the morning light, sits at the table drinking from a pint of cheap whiskey. Phil never looks at his son. Danny never takes his eyes off his father. After slipping a Pop-Tart into his book bag, Danny quietly exits through the backdoor.

EXT. RUTH'S HOUSE – DAY

As Danny pedals down the driveway, he encounters a small group of reporters who start pestering him with questions. His mother flies out the front door in her robe as Danny rides away. Ruth collars a female reporter in her mid-thirties, NONNIE.

> RUTH
> (exasperated)
> I thought a minor name's was kept confidential in these things.

> NONNIE
> (leaning close)
> He called us. I'm from the *Mondauk Common*. Nonnie Lelaina.

> RUTH
> Who called? Phil?

> NONNIE
> Danny.

> RUTH
> Danny called *you*? Why would he do that?

> NONNIE
> I don't know. He called my paper and the *Philadelphia Inquirer* too. Maybe a news station. I'm not sure. But word got around. Don't worry—no media outlet is going to release any personal information. Everyone's just looking for a quote. There aren't any photographers or news cameras here.

> RUTH
> What did he...when he called...what did Danny say?

> NONNIE
> He wanted to defend the teacher. He told us he wanted to buy her a Best Teacher Ever mug.

Ruth leans back against her front door as if she is going to faint. Nonnie blocks her from view and tries to steady her.

> NONNIE (CONT'D)
> Will you talk to me on the record? I wouldn't reveal your name or—

Ruth finds the door handle and backs into her house.

>   RUTH
>   (absently)
>   Later, later.

INT. POLICE STATION – DAY

>   DETECTIVE COTTEN
>   They're working on a plea deal? I thought the DA's office
>   said—

>   DETECTIVE WELLES
>   She's practically going to walk, partner. You'll see. I
>   overheard two women talking about the case in County
>   Hall yesterday. One said, "It was consensual," and the
>   other agreed, adding, "What was he gonna do? Turn it
>   down? My Billy would have been all over that."

EXT. FATHER HOSKINS HIGH – PARKING LOT – DAY

Danny sits on his bike watching the chattering crowd of students hanging around the front steps while they wait for school to start. The bell rings and soon Danny is alone. Moving slowly, he chains his bike and heads towards the steps.

INT. FATHER HOSKINS HIGH – HALLWAY #1 – DAY

Through Danny's eyes, he's in a walking fishbowl: everyone stares at him as he makes his way down the hall.

INT. FATHER HOSKINS HIGH – CLASSROOM #2 – DAY

Danny enters a noisy classroom before the teacher arrives, and it quiets down to whispers as he walks to his seat.

INT. FATHER HOSKINS HIGH – CAFETERIA – DAY

When Danny enters the cafeteria, a group of boys, led by Brendan, breaks into applause. A bunch of seniors hoot and holler and start singing "Maggie Mae." Danny sees Colin and Tommy sneak out through the doors on the opposite side.

Someone in Brendan's company throws a condom that hits Danny in the forehead. A deluge of ketchup packets and water bottle caps follow in its wake. Danny is stunned. *How does everyone know? From the news? But they said…*

BRENDAN
Tell us how she was, St. Clair! She taste as good as she—

MR. BOGLE, 49, the flinty vice-principal, pushes Brendan down in a chair and stuffs the end of the boy's tie in his surprised O of a mouth.

MR. BOGLE
Anyone else?

The noise subsides as Danny backs out of the cafeteria…

INT. FATHER HOSKINS HIGH – HALLWAY #2 – DAY

…right into Casey. Kids are pointing at him. A few boys clap him on the back, saying things like, "Way to go" and "I hope you gave it to her hard, St. Clair." Danny looks to Casey for help. She takes off her jeff cap and places it on his head, pulling the brim low.

CASEY
For a disguise.

He accepts it without a word although it's a little small for his head, and she escorts him out of the building, as he holds the cap in place.

EXT. FATHER HOSKINS HIGH – FRONT STEPS – DAY

The sun is shining, and Danny raises his face to it as he and Casey exit the school.

DANNY
Thank—

HIGH SCHOOL SENIOR #1
(from the bottom of the steps)
Look guys: it's DJ Jazzy Jeff Cap.

HIGH SCHOOL SENIOR #2
No, it's Sir Laid-a-Lot.

HIGH SCHOOL SENIOR #3
Isn't that the guy from *Sanford and Son?*

HIGH SCHOOL SENIOR #1
Who the fuck are Sanford and his son?

HIGH SCHOOL SENIOR #2
Looks like homeboy's got him a stable now: not just the
teach, but the über-dyke too. How *do* he do it?

HIGH SCHOOL SENIOR #3
Fred Sanford, he's got a junk yard, and Lamont, his son…

CASEY
(to Danny)
Come back and follow me. I know how to get out through
the janitor's—

DANNY
(to Casey)
Fuck you.

He takes off the jeff cap and throws it to the teasing seniors. As they toss it
back and forth, he runs past them and unchains his bike. Casey stands on
the steps and watches Danny pedal away.

HIGH SCHOOL SENIOR #1
(to Casey)
If we give this back to you, will you go down on my
girlfriend?

Casey stares at the boys until they toss the hat back, hitting her in the face.

INT. MONDAUK COUNTY COURT OF COMMON PLEAS –
JUDGE'S CHAMBERS – DAY

Lisa Ann pleads guilty to one count of institutional sexual assault. The judge
hands down a five-year suspended sentence and five years probation.

He informs Lisa Ann that her teaching certificate will be revoked and
instructs her that the conditions of her probation include registration as a
sex offender for fifteen years, treatment, avoidance of interaction, physical
or otherwise, with anyone under the age of eighteen, and absolutely no
further contact with the victim.

Holding back tears, Lisa Ann voices her assent when asked if she
understands the plea agreement and its implications. Her lawyer takes a
crumpled Kleenex from his pocket and offers it to her.

> NORMAN
> (whispering)
> It's clean.

> LISA ANN
> I'm not.

INT. POLICE STATION – DAY

> CAROL
> (sitting behind a very messy desk)
> Motherfuckers!

> DETECTIVE WELLES
> I told you. She didn't even get house arrest.

> CAROL
> I don't understand why the plea deal. You said she was
> talking.

> DETECTIVE COTTEN
> The witnesses were deemed weak, Danny wouldn't talk,
> and her ex's hired gun swooped in before we could nail
> down a confession.

Cotten takes out his pinky ball and bounces it off the wall. Carol catches it
and shoves it into a desk drawer.

CAROL

Not today, cowboy. I have tribal drums in my head. Once I decide to vacate your desk, you can retrieve your ball, yeah?

DETECTIVE WELLES

I swear it's like someone in the DA's office had a hard-on for Kavanagh.

DETECTIVE COTTEN

I'm hearing a lot of, "Where was she when I was fifteen?"

DETECTIVE WELLES

The father's a drunk tank regular, but at least the kid's got his mother.

CAROL

Have you met the mother?

INT. MARCIE'S HOUSE – LIVING ROOM – DAY

Through her binoculars, Marcie watches a cab pull up to the side of Lisa Ann's house.

INT. MONDCO CAB – DAY

LISA ANN

Let me off here, please. I never use the front door.

OLD CABBIE

A backdoor girl, huh? I heard about you. What? Too old for ya?

Lisa Ann tosses money at the cabbie and gets out.

OLD CABBIE (CONT'D)

Yeah, happy fuckin' Thanksgivin' to you too.

EXT. LISA ANN'S HOUSE – DAY

A group of reporters hustle to the back gate. Lisa Ann tries to ignore them as she makes her way to the backdoor.

> MALE REPORTER #1
> Lisa Ann, Lisa Ann!

> MALE REPORTER #2
> Do you think your sentence was just?

> MALE REPORTER #1
> Are the pregnancy rumors true? Are you really going to pose for *Playboy*?

> MALE REPORTER #3
> Any words for the victim's family?

> FEMALE REPORTER
> What will you do now, Mrs. Kavanagh?

Lisa Ann wearily turns around.

> FEMALE REPORTER (CONT'D)
> What else can—

> LISA ANN
> (her face drawn)
> What else is there? Nothing. There *was* nothing else.

INT. LISA ANN'S HOUSE – DAY

Lisa Ann sits at her dining room table sorting through a mountain of bills. When the reporters' chatter becomes a cacophony and their numbers seem to grow, she goes to the stereo and puts "Stephanie Says" by the Velvet Underground on repeat. Cranking the volume, she curls up on the sofa.

Her hand cautiously creeps under the cushions, and she is surprised when it returns clutching the yearbook. *The police didn't confiscate this?* She pages through it slowly as the song vibrates the walls.

INT. MARCIE'S HOUSE – NIGHT

Marcie has the binoculars to her eyes and the phone to her ear. The music from Lisa Ann's house is audible.

> MARCIE
> She's still at it, Cindy. Can you hear it? Been going on all day.

INT. LISA ANN'S HOUSE – LIVING ROOM – NIGHT

Lisa Ann is still curled up on the sofa, but the music is turned down. A table lamp offers a dim light as she talks on the phone.

> PAUL (V.O.)
> Are you alright?

> LISA ANN
> Yes. I just didn't want any visitors.

> PAUL (V.O.)
> I would have picked you up. I've been calling all—

> LISA ANN
> Thanks for keeping the lights on. It's like you knew I was coming home.

She shoves the yearbook back under the cushions.

> LISA ANN (CONT'D)
> I...I didn't even know if I *should* come home.
> (beat)
> Thank you for Fairlie, Paul. A divorce lawyer and now this. I'll pay you back.

> PAUL (V.O.)
> No need. You have enough bills. A law professor recommended—

> LISA ANN
> I barely got a slap on the wrist.

PAUL (V.O.)
The judge suspended the sentence. That's good.

LISA ANN
Because I'm not a predator, no—I'm a merit badge.

PAUL (V.O.)
Do you want me to come over?
(after a couple of beats)
Why, Lisa Ann? Why?

LISA ANN
Because I...
(beat)
We'll sort it out later.

PAUL (V.O.)
I'm here if you—

LISA ANN
(gently)
I know, Paul. I know.
(beat)
It didn't happen until after you left.

PAUL (V.O.)
Okay.

LISA ANN
I have to go.

She hangs up without saying goodbye.

LISA ANN (CONT'D)
(to herself)
Why? Because I'm in love with him. That's why, Paul.

She switches off the lamp.

LISA ANN (CONT'D)
At least I hope that's why

Using a remote, she turns the volume back up.

INT. RUTH'S HOUSE – KITCHEN – NIGHT

Phil drinks from a bottle of rye at the kitchen table as Ruth stands over him.

> RUTH
> It's a mystery, that's why. Since it happened, I've been trying to figure out how you're a part of this. How do you know her? Tell me that much.

> PHIL
> Just shut up. Leave me alone, will ya?

> RUTH
> Come on, Phil. How do you know her? She's a teacher— or was. She didn't dance in a strip club, and I don't think she was barhopping with Booker and Stan. You never went to one parent-teacher meeting. So how do you know her—because obviously you do?

Phil stands and pushes the table away. He reaches behind him, under his shirt, and grips the gun but releases it. He exits the room and clomps up the stairs. Ruth follows him.

INT. RUTH'S HOUSE – MASTER BEDROOM – NIGHT

Phil starts to throw clothes into a large overnight bag. As Ruth watches, he leaves the bedroom and returns with various toiletries.

> RUTH
> If you're going to leave right when Danny needs his father most, then be sure to take your condoms, the ones you hide in the garage behind the paint cans, and the Viagra you hide in your Tums bottle. Who are the Trojans for, I wonder? God knows you don't need rubbers with me anymore. I'm one and done, remember? No seed will find its purchase? Not that I'd fuck you even if there was a gun to my head. Maybe Roxy or Candy left you with a little itch, huh? And Viagra. Tsk, tsk, baby. Phillie not exactly coming up to bat? Wait—were you fucking the teacher too? That's it, isn't it? You were fuck—

Phil flinches.

> RUTH (CONT'D)
> No, that's not it at all, is it? I don't know how you know her, but you *wanted* to fuck her but couldn't, and your son did instead, and you can't deal with it because the only way you can get it up is by swallowing a little blue pill and having an underage tweaker play with your—

Phil goes to punch her but stops.

> RUTH (CONT'D)
> Go ahead. It's like you already have, so you might as well make it official. It would be the manliest thing you've done in a long time. I don't think whaling on your son really counts, but belting your wife because she knows you like the back of her hand, that's a true tough guy move. You'd be like Jake LaMotta but with erectile dysfunction.

> PHIL
> You're fuckin' crazy. You have a screw loose inside your dried up twat.

> RUTH
> You going to the teacher's now? How do you plan on getting past the reporters, the father of her—

> PHIL
> What the fuck you care?

He shoves her out of the way and exits.

EXT. OLDE BRIDGE – PENNYPACK CREEK – DAY

On an old iron bridge, Danny shares a joint with Brendan and Brendan's two scruffy friends. The bridge runs over a large creek and the road cuts through the woods. Except for the odd car, they are fairly alone this time of day. Brendan climbs up the bridge railing and begins walking along the ledge, holding onto to the bars. His friends follow his lead.

> BRENDAN
> (to Danny)
> You pussy? Pennypack Creek scare ya, make your balls wanna shrivel up?

Danny leans over and looks down at the swiftly moving and dirty creek. Casey skids her bike to a stop on the bridge next to Danny. She is wearing her jeff cap again.

> CASEY
> (to Danny)
> You don't have to do this. You don't have anything to prove.

> BRENDAN
> Look who it is, guys. You're lucky you're such a carpet muncher, or we'd pull a train on your skinny ass. Take ya in Pennypack Woods and shove a pinecone up your snatch.

> BRENDAN'S FRIEND #1
> Up your bitch wrinkle.

> BRENDAN'S FRIEND #2
> Your squish mitten.

> CASEY
> (to Danny, ignoring the other boys)
> It poured last night.

> DANNY
> So.

> CASEY
> So? That means the Pennypack's swollen. You fall in—

> BRENDAN
> What's it gonna be, ass master? You walkin' the line and puttin' some more hair on your chest or you gonna talk with k. d. lang all afternoon? You said if we got you high, you'd tell us all about Kavanagh's sweet poontang. We ain't heard diddly yet.

Danny looks conflicted, but after few tense moments, he knocks Casey's jeff cap off and turns to climb the railing. She picks up her cap and rides away looking confused and despondent.

INT. RUTH'S HOUSE – DAY

Ruth opens the door and lets Nonnie in. A reporter outside boos.

> RUTH
> Slow news day?

> NONNIE
> Sorry. He tailed me. It's just that nothing ever happens in Mondauk.

Nonnie follows Ruth into the kitchen.

> RUTH
> Would you like a cup of tea?

> NONNIE
> I'm more of a coffee girl usually, but yes, I would. Thank you.

> RUTH
> And my name won't be mentioned?

> NONNIE
> You'll be "the victim's mother." I'll use anonymous descriptions like that.

Ruth shoots the reporter a look of indignation.

EXT. THE BANKS OF PENNYPACK CREEK – DAY

Danny lies on his back on the red dirt, his clothes wet, obviously stoned. He is alone and whistling "Moondance." He looks at his watch: 4:35. He laughs and starts the song over.

EXT. CASEY'S BACKYARD – DAY

Casey stands over a stone barbecue pit with a lighter in one hand and her jeff cap in the other. She slowly moves the flame to the cap, close enough to singe the brim, but abruptly pulls the lighter away. She takes a deep breath and tries again but stops.

CASEY'S MOTHER (O.S.)
Casey! Dinner!

Casey regards at the jeff cap briefly, then throws the lighter in the barbecue pit. She shoves the cap into her jacket pocket and heads in for dinner.

INT. RUTH'S HOUSE – KITCHEN – DAY

Ruth and Nonnie sit at the kitchen table, a small tape recorder between them. Nonnie scribbles away on a steno pad.

RUTH
Isn't that enough?

NONNIE
It is if that's all you have to say. You see, Ruth, what you have here is an opportunity to strike a blow against the hypocrisy, the double-standard out there that describes what happens to a girl at the hands of a male teacher as molestation, sexual abuse, but often treats the corruption of a boy by a female educator as nothing more than the first notch on his belt. People in these situations—victims, their family members—don't often speak out, sometimes for very valid reasons, but their voices need to be heard. My paper's hasn't always been—

RUTH
(growing annoyed)
Isn't that what I'm doing now?

NONNIE
One boy described another's "encounter" with their female teacher as akin to "climbing Mt. Everest." I've been doing a lot of research for this piece, and there are leading psychologists who say that this type of abuse could leave a young male with a feeling of there being no boundaries. The effects, they say, don't often show up until their thirties or forties: addictive behaviors, compulsive disorders. They often end up in relationships defined by control. These women are no different than male offenders: Kavanagh's a predator, a bully. You have chance to stand up for—

RUTH
(raising her voice, appalled)
I don't want to stand up for anybody. I don't want to be
part of some kind of movement.

NONNIE
Not a movement. But here's the mother of a boy who's
been abused by—

RUTH
Was it abuse?

NONNIE
I'm sorry? What did you—

RUTH
The court, the police, Child Services: they called it
molestation. Despite what you said, Nonnie, I've yet to
witness this double standard. The authorities told me my
Danny was…they called it… But he's fifteen—and I
know, I know: he's still a child in many respects, but in
many ways, he's also a…I don't know. To be honest, I
don't understand men all that well. I wouldn't have fallen
for Phil's bullshit way back when if I did. And I
understand my son less and less every day.

NONNIE
But to say—

RUTH
He's not nine. He's not six. He's not three. He's fifteen.
His room smells like sweat and baby oil. There are socks
on his floor that stand straight up. And that's normal, I
know, or so I've read. I haven't caught him, thank God,
but his room is right above the kitchen. Sometimes his bed
rocks so hard, the light fixture above us actually swings.
More power to him. I just hope he doesn't run out of
spunk by the time he's old enough to want to use it for
something other than soiling my sheets. So he's an in-
between. Little boys don't masturbate morning, noon, and
night. In-betweens do. The word "teenager" to me implies
giggly girls not a young adult, and if he is a young adult,
why aren't we treating him like one instead of like a
helpless child.

NONNIE
(thrown)
But…you don't actually want me to write about this, do
you?

RUTH
Write about Danny's batting practices? I think you know
better. That was off the record or whatever you call it.
Other than that, write what you want. What I'm saying, all
I'm asking is: was it really molestation? Was it really…that
other word? I mean, I know it was wrong on certain
levels—the age difference, the imbalance of power—I just
don't know what I'd call it. You asked me earlier how I felt
about the teacher getting off easy, and what I said was the
truth: I never thought about it much. I just wanted Danny
to be okay. He made a decision. Is he impressionable?
Sure. But he's not stupid and he's not a toddler. He
certainly wasn't forced; it was consensual, despite what
anyone says. My Danny isn't a…he's not someone who
was preyed upon. So I just don't know if it was everything
the police said it was. I don't care about Lisa Ann
Kavanagh. I only care about Danny. But it appears I'm
losing more and more of him. Are you a parent, Nonnie?

NONNIE
(hesitant)
Mine's eight.

RUTH
One day he's clinging to your leg, the next he doesn't want
to know from you unless you're opening your wallet or
offering a ride.

NONNIE
(standing up and eyeing the light fixture)
I think that's everything, Ruth. Thank you for the tea and
thank you for—

RUTH
(laughing)
I thought he had a crush on the papergirl.

INT. MARCIE'S HOUSE – LIVING ROOM – DAY

> MARCIE
> (on the phone)
> It's all over the papers, what you said.

INT. RUTH'S HOUSE – KITCHEN – DAY

> RUTH
> (on the phone)
> And what did I say, Marcie, that half the town doesn't already think?

Marcie doesn't answer.

> RUTH (CONT'D)
> Oh God, I bet this got Cindy Drinkwater wet for the first time since the Reagan administration.

INTERCUT BETWEEN RUTH AND MARCIE

> MARCIE
> Ruth! I never!

> RUTH
> Did you call to talk about my interview or did you want something else?

> MARCIE
> I think—well, not just me; Addie Mae too—we were thinking maybe it's best if you don't come to Bookends and Bookmarks this month.

Ruth smiles widely.

> MARCIE (CONT'D)
> You're so much smarter than...you have an MA.

> RUTH
> I think when Addie Mae was little, it was all dirt floors and abacuses.

                    MARCIE
Plus Cora and Vera—well, they're so susceptible.
Discussing what we did about *The Crucible* is one thing, but
this newspaper article is a whole 'nother kettle of fish,
Ruth. And Adeline! I'm afraid she might—

                    RUTH
Did you really think I was coming back?

                    MARCIE
            (picking up her binoculars)
Ooh, she's coming out.

                    RUTH
Who's coming out?

EXT. HOLY REDEEMER HOSPITAL – PARKING LOT – NIGHT

Danny, Brendan, and Brendan's two seedy-looking friends from the bridge
huddle by the Emergency entrance. They are stoned. Brendan is holding a
bouquet of wilted flowers.

                    DANNY
        I don't get it.

                    BRENDAN
        What's to get, dipshit?

                    BRENDAN'S FRIEND #2
        Why do you keep him around? He don't tell us shit about
        the teacher.

                    BRENDAN'S FRIEND #1
        He don't even let us smell his fingers.

                    BRENDAN
        Will you both shut the fuck up? We've done this before.
        St. Clair hasn't. They might recognize us, but Danny Boy
        here, he's not known.

                    DANNY
        I don't understand.

> BRENDAN
>
> I told you I knew where we could get some really good
> shit, right?

> DANNY
>
> Yeah?

> BRENDAN
>
> Well, this is it, and visiting hours aren't over for another
> fifteen minutes.

Brendan leans down and whispers in Danny's ear.

INT. HOLY REDEEMER HOSPITAL – NIGHT

Danny slowly walks down a hallway carrying the wilted bouquet. He passes
several nurses and other hospital personnel. Nobody questions his
presence. He pokes his head into one room, then another. When he finds
an occupied, darkened room, he enters and starts hurriedly investigating the
IV bags. When the lights are turned on, he screams.

EXT. POLICE STATION – NIGHT

Ruth and Danny exit the station. Danny walks a couple of steps in front of
his mother.

INT. RUTH'S CAR – NIGHT

Ruth pulls into her driveway. A small group of reporters run towards the
car.

> RUTH
>
> (bitterly)
> What? The police blotter get published early? So much for
> anonymity.

Danny doesn't say anything.

> RUTH (CONT'D)
>
> If they start in on you, just—

Danny hops out and…

EXT. RUTH'S HOUSE – NIGHT

…makes his way to the house, enters, and slams the door behind him. Ruth tries to follow, but Nonnie grabs her arm.

NONNIE
The story made CNN!

Ruth goes to hit her but stops, taking in all the faces and cameras surrounding them.

RUTH
(in a barely controlled voice)
If I have to say it again, I'll have the police make you move. All of you: get off my lawn, get out of my driveway, and get off my fucking steps.
(to Nonnie)
And go to hell.

MALE REPORTER #1
Aw, Nonnie was just looking for a date with your—

Nonnie slaps the male reporter. Ruth finds she has to use her key to open the front door.

INT. POLICE STATION – NIGHT

Carol is sitting behind Cotten's desk again, using his computer, as the detective enters.

DETECTIVE COTTEN
Well, that was certainly a waste of time. I just cut Danny loose. He's not talking, and I don't blame him. It's no surprise Danny's acting out, but I don't know if taking him from his mother is the best way to go here.

CAROL
Okay, fine, yeah. Do you know this whole time not one paper used the words "sexual assault" unless reporting the initial charges or her plea deal? They all used soft

euphemisms like "inappropriate behavior." The *City Paper* actually wrote that Kavanagh "took liberties with the student."

Cotten begins to speak, but Carol rises out of the chair and places a finger on his lips, then puts her hand out. The detective gives her the pinky ball.

> CAROL (CONT'D)
> I'm on a tear, Cotten. Ride the wave or get the hell out of the way. All Kavanagh has to do is write "I promise not to touch children" a hundred times on the blackboard to avoid prison. The mother puts up a rousing, puzzling defense of her son in the paper. "My boy's not a victim," she declares. *No one believes this kid was assaulted.* My bailiff buddy told me even the judge acted as if Kavanagh was the chick from the "Hot for Teacher" video.

> DETECTIVE COTTEN
> They fail to see—

> CAROL
> ...how this is not fucking normal? "A victimless crime," I heard someone say. "Boys will be boys." Wink, wink. Does anyone listen to themselves? *Boys!* "There wasn't any violence, so what's the problem?" But there will be violence, Cotten. It's just been deferred. When this boy becomes a man and that badge of honor becomes a burden of shame, all that built-up anger will need a place to go—and *boom!*

Carol covers her eyes with her hands. Cotten goes to pat her back but thinks better of it.

> CAROL (CONT'D)
> No one looks at this situation like that—not the mother, who's currently orbiting Jupiter, certainly not Kavanagh, who believes we just don't understand: she did this because they're in love. Pah!

She turns the chair around and starts throwing the pinky ball against the wall.

> CAROL (CONT'D)
> There was little risk of rejection. She crossed the line to

satisfy herself, coloring her crime with the hues and perfumes of romance. If the genders were reversed, the villagers would've strung up the guy by his balls already.

She throws the pinky ball with extra force, and it flies over her head. A crashing sound follows. No one in the immediate area reacts; it's as if they are used to this sort of thing.

> DETECTIVE COTTEN
>
> You got a way of saying *balls* that makes me forget everything *except* my balls. You wanna get a drink, leave that hellhole of a desk for a while? I'm buying.

> CAROL
>
> This is *your* hellhole of a desk, cowboy. But thanks, I have to pass. I need to go home, take a long, hot shower, and wash this town right out of my hair.

> DETECTIVE COTTEN
>
> You're right: your idea sounds better. Got an extra shower cap?

EXT. RUTH'S HOUSE – DAY

Ruth's sister, EMILY, 40, stands on the front steps surveying all the footprints on the lawn. She is conservatively dressed, her hair is pulled back, and her countenance is severe—a dour Mary Poppins. Ruth opens the door, a tight smile on her face.

INT. RUTH'S HOUSE – LIVING ROOM – DAY

Ruth and Emily are drinking tea.

> RUTH
> (lightly sarcastic)
> Wow.

> EMILY
> It's for the best, Ruth.

> RUTH
> What it takes to get my big sister out of Reading.

EMILY

They may remove the boy from your home. You said so
yourself.

RUTH

So the social worker told me. Carol. I used to sort of like
her. Not so much now. You know, every time I've met
with her, she was wearing the same suit. You think she
only has one or...

EMILY

It's what you said in the newspaper more than anything.
Daniel's drug arrest at the hospital didn't help, but what
you told that reporter raised all kinds of red flags.

RUTH

You'd think I was pimping him out, all this nonsense. I
just didn't want him to feel bad about...to end up with
Phil's victim mentality.

EMILY

Yet the article felt like it was really all about Ruth St. Clair.

RUTH

Fuck you.

EMILY

You called me, Ruth. At least you'll know where he is.
(exasperated but trying not to show it)
Just until the end of the term. Then in the summer, he can
decide—

Ruth begins to cry.

RUTH

(whispering)
Take him. Take him till the end of the school year.

Emily looks triumphant. Neither notices Danny at the bottom of the stairs
until he speaks.

DANNY

(to Emily)
I don't want to go to Reading.

EMILY
(as if speaking to someone much
younger)
But you don't want to go to a group home, now, do you,
Daniel? You can have Johnny's old room.
(to Ruth)
He's interning in DC now.

DANNY
I don't even know where Reading is!

EMILY
Daniel, there is a great school right—

DANNY
(yelling)
Danny! My name is Danny!

Emily turns to Ruth who looks away.

RUTH
(to Danny in a quiet, quivering voice)
Reading's not so bad. We grew up there. They have a
minor league hockey team—right, Em? You like ice
hockey, Danny. There's a great museum and they have a
planetarium. Oh, and there are air shows at—

As Ruth talks, Danny takes the small framed family photograph off the
wall. After studying it for a moment, he throws it at Ruth but misses her.

DANNY
(to Emily)
I'll be outside. Is your car unlocked?

He exits without waiting for an answer. Ruth stands up and heads to the
kitchen.

RUTH
The suitcases are upstairs.

INT. THE BLUE COMET – NIGHT

Lisa Ann walks into the bar apprehensively. They are only a few patrons; no one notices her. Nicky is at the end of the bar reading a racing form. He doesn't look up as she approaches.

> NICKY
>
> My mother used to say it was one of those—what d'ya call 'em?—continuum lines: in a pickle; behind the eight ball; up to your neck in it; screwed, blewed, and tattooed; dead meat; and fucked. Congrats, Lisey: you've just attained the supreme level of totally fucked.

> LISA ANN
>
> Nicky...

> NICKY
> (looking up)
> Guess you'll be wantin' extra hours.

Lisa Ann smiles and nods.

INT. FATHER HOSKINS HIGH – LOCKER ROOM – DAY

Casey stands in front of an open, empty locker—Danny's. She fingers the Green Day sticker on the inside of the door. Angrily, she tries to scrape it off and succeeds in removing a large portion. She isn't wearing her jeff cap.

INT. ASSUMPTION RECTORY – WAITING ROOM – DAY

Ruth sits looking at the religious art. Her eyes catch a Madonna and child, and she looks away. An older woman, GRACE, sits behind a small desk, spraying Windex on the phone. She is startled when it rings and begins pushing buttons. Windex drips off the handset.

> GRACE
>
> Assumption of Our Lady Rectory. Can you hear me? Still wet, please hold.

When Father Dave enters the small waiting room, Ruth jumps up, as does Grace.

FATHER DAVE

Ruth! How good to see you. Come. I hope I didn't keep you waiting long.

INT. ASSUMPTION RECTORY – PASTOR'S OFFICE – DAY

Father Dave offers Ruth a chair before taking his place behind a tidy desk.

FATHER DAVE

Coffee?

RUTH

No thank you. I'm a tea drinker.

FATHER DAVE

I think there's Earl Grey around here somewhere. Let me buzz Grace.

RUTH

That won't be necessary, Father. This isn't…I mean…

FATHER DAVE

It's not a social call? It rarely is. Chess with Mr. Bogle on occasion, but—

RUTH

I didn't know who else to—

FATHER DAVE

Say no more.

RUTH

I know I haven't been to church in a while, but—

FATHER DAVE

Past is past. Hit the confessional, and the slate's clean— long as you mean it, of course. That's how we get repeat customers, Ruth. Tie one on Friday night, confess Saturday afternoon. Lather, rinse, repeat.

RUTH

It's just…Danny…my Danny left. He moved to Reading with my—

                    FATHER DAVE
I know all about it, my child.

Ruth raises her eyebrows—*my child?*

                FATHER DAVE (CONT'D)
Marcie Dietlin's a chatterbox. Ditto for Addie Mae
Browne.

                        RUTH
At least the house is quieter.
                    (cringing)
I don't want confession, Father. I just don't know what to
do. Phil, well—not that I care where he went—but he's,
Christ, God knows where—sorry.

                    FATHER DAVE
God knows where Phil is, Ruth.

                        RUTH
Yeah, well, I hope He's keeping a close eye on the bastard.
Sorry again.

                    FATHER DAVE
You calls 'em as you sees 'em.

                        RUTH
                    (standing up)
Maybe this was a mistake. I don't know what I was looking
for. Some lightning bolt from the sky or—

                    FATHER DAVE
That's Zeus. The lightning bolt. Ours usually sends an
angel.

                        RUTH
Angels and catastrophic floods.

                    FATHER DAVE
One little Earth-covering flood, and it's all anyone ever
remembers. Listen, Ruth, the Church is here for you in
whatever way we can be. I can refer you to several
excellent therapists, or you can simply meet with a priest
on a regular basis. We'll find your path again. God didn't

create one for you just to abandon construction partway
through.

RUTH
(sitting again)
I don't know...why don't I just talk to...can't I just talk to
you?

FATHER DAVE
If only that were so, my child.

RUTH
(furrowing her brow: *my child* again?)
It's just that I know you, but I'm sure as pastor your plate's
pretty full.

FATHER DAVE
(picking up the phone)
Yes, but that's not the reason. I have to go out of town for
a conference. But you just wait here, and I'll track down
Father Sailor or Father Curran.

RUTH
Aren't they a little...?

FATHER DAVE
Old? Well, they didn't know Christ personally, but let's just
say... I have an idea. Our new seminarian. He'll be
ordained a deacon next year. I'm pretty sure he's still
around today. You'll like him.

RUTH
Didn't you say he was kind of young?

FATHER DAVE
Yes, but we don't have any young priests. I'm as young as
they come in these here parts, so let me...
(into the phone)
Grace? Track down Mr. Donati for me, will you? Well,
then just *dry* it.

INT. ASSUMPTION RECTORY – LIBRARY – DAY

Ruth and ROMAN DONATI, the seminarian, 26, sit in comfortable chairs in a cramped room surrounded by books. Roman has dark hair and a strong face with a mouth given to wide smiles. They are drinking tea.

> ROMAN
> Just call me Roman, please. Every time I hear Mr. Donati, I smell feet.

> RUTH
> Feet?

> ROMAN
> My father was a cobbler.

Ruth returns Roman's smile.

> ROMAN (CONT'D)
> This is the beginning of my third year in seminary. St. Robert Bellarmine in Wynnewood. I've been assigned to Assumption for my internship. I'm here most weekends plus Wednesdays if my schedule allows. Last chance for a slow dance, I call it.

> RUTH
> Oh?

> ROMAN
> After the spring semester, I'll take a vow of celibacy and be ordained a deacon, then after I graduate, a priest. Ordination is forever, so even if a priest were to lose the clerical state, he is to remain celibate.
> (beat)
> If my little joke was in any way—

> RUTH
> I quite liked it. It takes a lot to give up the ol' slow dance, I imagine.

> ROMAN
> This is going to sound odd, but I've known since I was in grade school that I was being called to the priesthood.

                    RUTH
And how did a grade-schooler come to know this?

                    ROMAN
I collected holy cards instead of baseball cards. Funeral
cards too.

                    RUTH
          (laughing)
Let me tell you: you're a card, alright. Me, I always thought
I would be a teacher. Got my master's, even did my
student teaching. But somehow I ended up heading the
underwriting department at a TPA. *Health benefit plan risk
management.* Sounds as dry as a dead camel, but it's not all
bad. I telecommute a lot which makes for pretty flexible
hours. So…if you always knew your calling, why the last
chance for a slow dance?

As they talk, they move up to the edge of their chairs, hands gesticulating.

                    ROMAN
A case of pre-wedding jitters, nothing more. If it was
something I actually considered doing, this year would be
my last chance to back out before I marry myself to God.

                    RUTH
Marriages end.

                    ROMAN
That's the spirit. Sow doubt in the seminarian.

                    RUTH
My apologies. My job is to assess risks. I look for weak
spots.

                    ROMAN
In yourself too?

                    RUTH
Nice transition.

                    ROMAN
I'm learning.

She touches his knee. Neither comment on the static electricity.

> RUTH
>
> I don't have to look for weak spots in myself.

> ROMAN
>
> Oh, no?

> RUTH
>
> The light shines right through me.

> ROMAN
>
> And through us all. But that's not what you meant.

> RUTH
>
> No. I don't even know if I believe in God anymore. In college, I cut my teeth on Kierkegaard and—

> ROMAN
>
> Ah, ol' Søren.

> RUTH
>
> …yeah, and Bertrand Russell with—

> ROMAN
>
> "Religion is based, I think, primarily and mainly upon fear."

> RUTH
>
> …right, with a healthy dash of Joseph Campbell—and nice quote there, Bartlett.

> ROMAN
>
> Campbell, you'll get no argument from me there. *The Power of Myth* is one of my favorite books. But you said, "the light shines right through me." Do you mean you're like Dazzler or do you mean you're full of holes?

> RUTH
>
> Dazzler?

> ROMAN
>
> Superhero. She was a mutant who could convert sonic vibrations into light and laser beams. But I suppose light

didn't shine *through* her; it emanated *from* her. Dazzler had her own Marvel comic in the early '80s. Forty-two issues.

RUTH

So *that's* what you do after lights out in seminary.

ROMAN

Comic book geek as a kid. Holy cards weren't the only things I collected.

RUTH

Well, I'm more Swiss cheese than superheroine.

Roman tilts his head. Ruth stares for a second or two, then looks away.

RUTH (CONT'D)

What I meant was that light shines through me because I have so many weak spots.

ROMAN

But we all do.

RUTH

If you say "my child," I'll stomp on your foot.

ROMAN

All of us are stained with sins, Mrs. St. Clair, and that makes us feel less than whole.

RUTH

My drunk, cheating husband has left—which isn't necessarily a bad thing. My son has just lost his virginity to his social studies teacher, and he's been spirited away by my sister, who, since her husband died, has become a Super Catholic—like Cindy Drinkwater but with better hair and breath. How many people's weak spots cause others to sin or to be removed from your presence? Because, I'll tell you, Roman, I don't know too many. I've met evil people. I know manipulative people. But have you ever run into someone with powers like mine in all your Gospels and comic books?

ROMAN

That's not quite the way it works, Mrs. St. Clair, not for—

> RUTH
>
> It's Ruth.

> ROMAN
>
> Ruth.

> RUTH
>
> Super Ruth.

> ROMAN
>
> Dazzler.

INT. RUTH'S HOUSE – KITCHEN – NIGHT

> RUTH
> (on the phone)
> Roman. What does it matter to you?

> MARCIE (V.O.)
> The deacon! You've met him? What's he like?

> RUTH
> Like a mailman without mail. And he's not a deacon, not
> yet.

> MARCIE (V.O.)
> I don't…mailman? Ruth, you'll have to explain that to—

> RUTH
> I have to go. Bye.

Ruth hangs up, bites her lip, and stares at the kitchen table. On it is a bag
from Brave New Worlds Comics next to three old *Dazzler* issues in clear
bags.

INT. EMILY'S HOUSE – DANNY'S ROOM – NIGHT

Danny sits on a carefully made bed. There are old baseball pennants on the
walls, a Bible on the nightstand, and a crucifix above the bed. He fiddles
around with an old, small AM-FM transistor radio until he finds some
rock'n'roll. He holds it to his ear as if listening for a secret message.

INT. EMILY'S HOUSE – UPSTAIRS HALLWAY – NIGHT

Emily goes to knock on Danny's door but stops when she catches snatches of the radio's tinny output. She covers her mouth, caught unawares in a wave of nostalgia, then moves on.

INT. ASSUMPTION RECTORY – LIBRARY – DAY

Ruth and Roman are seated as before, sipping tea.

> ROMAN
> Our third time. I must be a good listener.

> RUTH
> You're counting?

> ROMAN
> No, I—

> RUTH
> It would have been four times but you went back early last Sunday. And, yes, you're that good. Good enough for Cindy Drinkwater to tail me today.

> ROMAN
> Oh my. Small town intrigue. Mondauk Proper seems to thrive on it.

> RUTH
> All of Mondauk County does. Cindy's nothing to worry about. Bernadette Fuller and the lay Faith Board—they're trouble. The National Socialist Catholic Party. But Cindy and her goody-two-shoes guild? They may have a foothold on the Faith Board, but ultimately, they're like groupies for priests.

> ROMAN
> Well, we *are* the ecclesiastical rock stars.

> RUTH
> For that crowd, priests are the ecclesiastical Rat Pack. But let's not forget: you're not a cleric. Not yet.

ROMAN

Not yet is right. Just a lowly third year seminarian.

RUTH

Last chance for a slow dance.

ROMAN

I do believe my dance card's filled.

RUTH

You told me that you always knew you were going to be called, but why do you *want* to be a priest? I mean, there has to be some free will in this, divine calling or not.

ROMAN
(after a moment of reflection)

Have you ever fallen for someone so hard, Ruth, that you can't help but give everything else up even if it means having to suffer? Even if it means possibly not being loved back? For isn't that faith? Faith isn't an absence of doubt. Doubt's an essential ingredient. And if you can give something up and not suffer, then you really haven't given up anything of value. Like all those people during Lent, giving up Cheez-Its and snickerdoodles. It has to hurt in order to wake you up to the fact that faith sometimes requires sacrifice. So…I gave myself up. I gave up my family to some extent, I gave up—

RUTH

Sex.

ROMAN
(laughing)

That's right. Sex. And don't ask if I ever dipped my beak back in the day, 'cause I'm not squawking.

RUTH

You talk about holy orders like a lot of people talk about sex. I figure your beak must have been damp once or twice.

ROMAN

After a while, you don't even miss missing it.

                    RUTH
It's not too late. You haven't signed the papers yet.

                    ROMAN
I'm not sure God would see it that way.

                    RUTH
I think God would want to see you happy—however
you're happy.

She lightly touches his hand, but Roman pulls it away.

                RUTH (CONT'D)
            (standing up)
        I think I should go.

Roman takes her hand and gently pulls her back to her chair.

                    ROMAN
Don't go. Not just yet.

EXT. ASSUMPTION RECTORY – DAY

Ruth exits the rectory. As she walks to her car, Cindy Drinkwater appears
and takes hold of her arm.

                    CINDY
I don't know what you think you're doing, but you're not
going to get away with it.

                    RUTH
            (pulling her arm free)
        I certainly hope not.

INT. EMILY'S HOUSE – UPSTAIRS HALLWAY – NIGHT

Danny listens to the sound of the television coming from the first floor.
Satisfied, he sneaks down the hall to...

INT. EMILY'S HOUSE – EMILY'S ROOM – NIGHT

...Emily's room. In the dark, he picks up the phone but pauses as if he's unsure who to call or why. He listens to the tone and doesn't hang up until it turns into beeping.

INT. EMILY'S HOUSE – BATHROOM – NIGHT

Danny paws through the contents of the medicine cabinet, but the most dangerous item he finds is a pink Lady Bic. He tries to break the plastic to get to the razor but succeeds only in snapping off the handle. Frustrated, he throws the pieces in the sink and empties a small bottle of aspirin into his hand as Emily opens the door.

Without a word, she upturns his hand over the toilet and dumps the aspirin. As she places the broken pieces of the Lady Bic in a tissue, Danny moves out of her way and notices a *second* Lady Bic on the edge of the tub, partially obscured by the shower curtain. Emily begins to straighten up and reorder the medicine cabinet. All of this happens while she speaks.

> EMILY
> You know, Daniel, your Uncle Charlie, he was a real music hound. That big cabinet in the dining room? It's stuffed with vinyl. You know what records are? Well, that turntable in the basement works. If you like, you can bring it up to your room. Why don't you go take a look? Go on. I'll finish up here.

Danny exits.

INT. EMILY'S HOUSE – DINING ROOM – NIGHT

Danny slides open the doors of a long wooden floor cabinet and runs his fingers along the spines of Uncle Charlie's vinyl collection. He pulls out a few. *Tommy* by the Who. Elvis Presley's debut album. *Music from Big Pink* by the Band. *Moondance* by Van Morrison. He holds the last one up and stares at the cover, then quickly heads to the basement.

INT. EMILY'S HOUSE – BATHROOM – NIGHT

Emily finishes cleaning up. Suddenly the strains of "And It Stoned Me," the first cut on *Moondance*, floats up from the basement. Emily shudders, straightens a towel, and turns off the bathroom light.

INT. ASSUMPTION RECTORY – HALLWAY – DAY

Ruth and Roman exit the library.

> ROMAN
> …and as soon as Mrs. Martucci, the housekeeper, comes back from vacation, Father Dave said they'll clean it out so I'll have—

> RUTH
> Mrs. Martucci isn't here today?

> ROMAN
> No, no one's here right now. Pastoral care and—

Ruth reaches up and kisses him softly on the lips, taking her time. It is a closed-mouth kiss, but it crackles with energy all the same.

> ROMAN (CONT'D)
> (when the kiss is finished)
> I can't.

> RUTH
> You just did.

She walks down the hall, opens the door, and exits into the sunlight. Roman reaches up and gently touches his lips.

EXT. THE BLUE COMET – NIGHT

The signs are turned off, and the employees exit the Comet. Nicky walks Lisa Ann across the street. Phil watches from the alley again.

> LISA ANN
> I'm just down the street here.

> NICKY
> You alright? Busy night.

LISA ANN

I'll be fine. Just beat. With Darla calling out... Well, I hate flying solo—even on a weeknight.

NICKY

Yeah. Okay, be careful.
            (as he walks back across the street)
Hey, Lisey, what's the difference between erotic and kinky?

LISA ANN
            (sighing)
I don't know, Nicky: what's the difference between erotic and kinky?

NICKY

Erotic is usin' a feather. Kinky is usin' the whole chicken.

He laughs long and hard as he reaches the opposite pavement and turns the corner. Lisa Ann shakes her head. As she nears the alley, Phil slinks into the shadows. When he hears her car door slam and the engine start, he creeps out. As she drives away without seeing him, he shapes his fingers into a gun, points at her car, and shoots.

PHIL

Pow.

INT. SEVENTH HEAVEN— DAY

Phil joins Stan, Shelley, and Booker at a table. The three men are watching Jewels pole dance to George Michael's "Father Figure." They are quite drunk.

PHIL
I'm gonna kill that bitch.

STAN
            (pointing to Jewels)
That bitch?

BOOKER
Please not that bitch.

Phil glares at Booker.

SHELLEY
(to Booker)
You're gonna get bitch slapped again.

STAN
(pointing again to Jewels)
Son of a bitch. *That* bitch?

BOOKER
Shut your bitch hole.

SHELLEY
Always beatin' his bitch flaps and never goin' anywhere.

STAN

Bitch, please.

BOOKER
Both of you give me a headache: you with your bitch tits
and you, Shel, with your bitch logic.

STAN
Don't bitch me out because of Shelley.

BOOKER
Listen to him: gettin' all bitchy.

SHELLEY
(nodding towards Jewels)
Phil here ain't talkin' about that bitch and chips.

STAN
Well, if he was, I'd understand: she's a bitch and a half.

BOOKER
Who's he bitchin' about then?

SHELLEY
Who do you think, you son of a female dog? His wife.
He's been livin' at the Hub Motel, for Christ's sake.

Jewels, her back to the patrons, starts moving her head so that her long
black hair spins.

PHIL
(staring at the dancer)
I'm gonna kill that motherfuckin' bitch.

BOOKER
Is Shel right, Philly? Your wife.

PHIL
(to himself, still staring at Jewels)
Looks just like her from the back.
(to Booker)
My wife? Don't you know? Her pussy's already dead.

INT. RUTH'S HOUSE – UPSTAIRS BATHROOM – DAY

After Ruth fusses with her hair, she applies lipstick but wipes it off.

RUTH
(staring into the mirror)
I suppose saying the "Our Father" would be inappropriate
at this juncture.

INT. ASSUMPTION RECTORY – WAITING ROOM – DAY

Grace won't meet Ruth's eyes and her greeting is perfunctory. Father Dave
comes out to shake hands with a confused Ruth, who peers behind the
pastor.

FATHER DAVE
Ruth! Won't you come in?

RUTH
It's…no…I was just…
(laughing nervously)
I was just looking for Roman, Pastor.

FATHER DAVE
Then I think you should come in.

RUTH
I'd just as soon you tell me out here.

FATHER DAVE

Okay.
>   (beat)
Roman left.

Ruth bites her lower lip and looks caught between a sigh of relief and a scream: this is a pass from a situation so wrong, but it could have been her chance at a new life.

RUTH

Where did he...where did he go?

Father Dave walks back into his office, and Ruth follows but only as far as the doorway.

INT. ASSUMPTION RECTORY – PASTOR'S OFFICE – DAY

FATHER DAVE

Back to St. Bellarmine. Back to the seminary. Then on to—

RUTH

Ordination? But...the last chance for a slow dance.

FATHER DAVE

I'm sorry? No, he's not getting ordained to the diaconate, not...

RUTH
>   (overlapping)
He left the...he left the Church?

FATHER DAVE

...until the end of the spring term. Left? Oh no, my child. It's just that after many hours of prayer, he requested a transfer to another parish where he could finish his internship. He really wanted to serve an inner city parish. He went back to stay at the seminary while his transfer is being processed. It's been more or less approved, but he felt staying here might—

RUTH

Might what?

                    FATHER DAVE
Oh, it's nothing we need be concerned about. I'm here,
and you and I can talk it out, maybe see if we can't get you
back to Mass on Sundays.

                    RUTH
Might what, Father?

                    FATHER DAVE
          (after a beat)
Might succumb to temptation of some sort.
          (poking through the mail on his desk)
I get more offers to lower my mortgage, as if…
          (beat)
Might succumb to the temptation of living in a small
suburban town, I suppose. It *can* be quite comfortable
here.

Shaken, Ruth turns to go.

                    FATHER DAVE (CONT'D)
Cindy Drinkwater and her God Squad, they don't know
Roman left—yet. Bernadette Fuller and the Faith Board
don't even know, but I'm going to have to inform them
shortly, which will mean Bernadette will tell—

                    RUTH
I understand. Thank you, Father.

Ruth exits.

                    FATHER DAVE
May God bless you, Ruth St. Clair.

INT. THE BLUE COMET – DAY

Christmas lights decorate the bar. Pre-happy hour, the place is sparsely
populated, but Frank and his two senior cronies, OREO, who dips Oreo
cookies into his whiskey and ROCCO, who appears to be asleep sitting up,
are in their usual places. Nicky is at the far end moving a toothpick from
one side of his mouth to the other as he works on a crossword puzzle.

NICKY

Frank, six letter word meaning "to break a promise or commitment."

FRANK
(slurring and swaying)
Renege.

NICKY

You besotted bastard, how do you do it?

FRANK

You dunderheaded squat rack, it's a matter of degrees.

Lisa Ann walks in and Nicky taps his watch.

LISA ANN

Sorry! Hey, where's Deb, Nicky? I thought I was closing with her.

NICKY

Lisey, listen: I gotta put you on mostly day shifts—by yourself. I'll be here to help out, and I'll pour with you tonight too. I'll even be your barback during the day since we don't have anyone for afternoons right now.

LISA ANN

I don't understand. I make more money at night. I need to—

NICKY

None of the girls…they—

FRANK

Just tell her already: none of 'em wanna work witcha, lady.

LISA ANN

Nicky?

NICKY

The girls, they just don't feel…comfortable.

FRANK

A Southern Comfortable! That's what I want.

> LISA ANN
> And me, Nicky? How do you think I feel? Do you think I feel comfortable?

> FRANK
> You got me and the boss man, sweetie pie.

> ROCCO
> (waking up and singing)
> " 'Cause that's what friends are for…keep smiling, keep shining…"

After a beat, Lisa Ann sticks her purse behind the bar and heads to the bathroom, trying to wipe away her tears as fast they come. Nicky flicks his toothpick at Frank's head.

INT./EXT. RUTH'S CAR – DAY

Ruth drives up a long driveway and pulls into a parking lot at St. Robert Bellarmine Seminary. The radio is blasting: "The problem is all inside your head, she said to me…" When Ruth gets out, she is confronted by a discomforting silence.

EXT./INT. ST. ROBERT BELLARMINE SEMINARY – DAY

Ruth walks up a path to an imposing grey stone building topped with a bell tower and enters. With her shoes clicking loudly on the marble floor, Ruth approaches the front desk.

> DEACON BEHIND DESK
> Good afternoon. May I help you?

Ruth opens her mouth but nothing comes out.

> DEACON BEHIND DESK (CONT'D)
> Ma'am? May I be of some assistance?

Ruth frantically looks this way and that.

> DEACON BEHIND DESK (CONT'D)
> (picking up the phone)
> Can I get you some water? Ma'am? Is there something I
> can do to—

> RUTH
> I'm running out of time.

She quickly turns and exits.

INT. THE BLUE COMET – DAY

Six patrons sit at the bar, including Frank's trio. Nicky reads *Muscle Car Review* at the far end. Lisa Ann is the sole bartender. The cook writes the specials on the chalkboard.

> LISA ANN
> I swear, it feels like someone is following me.

> NICKY
> You got nothin' to worry about, darlin'. Not when I'm
> around.

> LISA ANN
> I just wish whatever was going to happen would happen
> already, so I can get on with my life—or not.

> NICKY
> Hey, Lisey, when does a Cub Scout become a Boy Scout?

> LISA ANN
> I know we're a little slow but…okay, Nicky: when does a
> Cub Scout become a Boy Scout?

> NICKY
> When he eats his first Brownie!

He brays and some men at the bar join in. Oreo struggles to open an Oreo.

> FRANK
> (slurring)
> Which sexual position produces the ugliest children?

A middle-aged woman enters the bar holding a notebook.

> LISA ANN
>
> Okay, Frank, which…

> NICKY
> (to Lisa Ann, overlapping)
>
> Don't.

> LISA ANN
>
> …sexual position produces the ugliest children?

> FRANK
>
> I don't know. Ask your mom.

The old man laughs but stops to adjust his teeth.

> MIDDLE-AGED WOMAN
>
> Excuse me.

Nicky gets up, smoothes his jacket and hair, and walks over.

> NICKY
>
> Can I get you a table?

> MIDDLE-AGED WOMAN
>
> I'm looking for Lisa Ann Kavanagh.

Lisa Ann turns her back to the woman and faces the cash register.

> NICKY
>
> She ain't here.

> MIDDLE-AGED WOMAN
>
> Oh, that's too bad, I—

> FRANK
> (pointing)
>
> She's right there.

> NICKY
>
> Regular Henry Hill, this guy.
> (leaning towards Frank's ear)
> No more buy-backs for you, pal.

                        FRANK
Booze flows like mud around here anyway.

Lisa Ann turns around.

                        LISA ANN
Are you a reporter or from Publisher's Clearing House?

                        OREO
                    (slurring)
You may already be a winner.

                        MIDDLE-AGED WOMAN
I'm a journalist, and—

                        NICKY
                (escorting the woman towards the door)
No press allowed, thank you.

                        LISA ANN
                (clearly tired but talking as if she deserves this)
No, it's okay, Nicky. Let her go. One question. Ask away.

                        OREO
Make it a good one.

Nicky smacks Frank on the back of his head. Frank adjusts his teeth again.

                        MIDDLE-AGED WOMAN
Oh goody. Just let me get my pen.

She reaches into her purse, pulls out an egg, and tosses it at Lisa Ann. She
misses, and the egg splatters across the rows of bottles behind the bar.

                        MIDDLE-AGED WOMAN (CONT'D)
Child molester! You're going to burn in hell! Pedophile!

Nicky picks the woman up and uses her body to open the door. Lisa Ann
gets a rag and starts wiping down the bottles.

                        FRANK
In-eggs-pert eggs-ecution.

OREO

Cool it, Frankie. Have a cookie.

FRANK

(hissing at Lisa Ann)

Eggs-anthema subitum!

Nicky, back from tossing out the reporter, smacks Frank on the back of his head again, and the old man's uppers fall out of his mouth onto the bar as the other patrons groan.

NICKY

Between the girls and her, Lisey, clearly not everyone thinks you're a faculty pinup. I'd say your reviews are mixed.

INT. RUTH'S HOUSE – KITCHEN – NIGHT

Ruth is on the phone with Emily. During the call, Ruth's mood fluctuates wildly, from agitation and nervousness to sincerity and even relief, often at inappropriate times.

RUTH

But—

INT. EMILY'S HOUSE – EMILY'S ROOM – NIGHT

EMILY

(filing her nails)

Ruth, he won't come to the phone.

INTERCUT BETWEEN RUTH AND EMILY

RUTH

But—

EMILY

I asked him twice. He won't.

RUTH

How...how's he getting along? How's he—?

                              EMILY
Ruth—

                              RUTH
Is he adjusting to school? Has he made new friends?

                              EMILY
I think for now it's best the less you know the better. Let
the boy settle in.

EMILY'S HOUSE – BATHROOM

Occurs simultaneously with the overlapping phone conversation between
Ruth and Emily:

Danny takes a cautious step out of the dark bathroom clutching a Lady Bic.

INTERCUT BETWEEN RUTH AND EMILY

                              RUTH
                          (disgusted)
The boy. Danny, you mean.

                              EMILY
                    (sighing dramatically)
Yes, Daniel. He needs to get acclimated.

                              RUTH
                    (suddenly on the alert)
And why is that, Em? If he's just staying until the end of
the school year—

Emily stops filing her nails and gives the phone conversation her undivided
attention.

                              EMILY
Remember how you suddenly started going on and on
about having a baby? Probably to keep you company, I
thought, since Phil was already busy holding up the bar. Or
maybe you thought a baby would save your marriage.

                        RUTH
                (barely above a whisper)
I wanted to start someone else's story since mine seemed
already over.

                       EMILY
But as soon as you became pregnant and even after Daniel
was born, it was obvious you had such mixed feelings
about his existence in your life. All you talked about were
varicose veins. You didn't even name him for ten days.

                        RUTH
I was terrified of being caught between the pages of
someone else's story.

EMILY'S HOUSE – DANNY'S ROOM

Occurs simultaneously with overlapping phone conversation:

Danny opens a desk drawer of school supplies and sticks the Lady Bic in a
box of pens, which he shoves to the back. He sits on his bed, chin in hand,
and stares at the drawer.

INTERCUT BETWEEN RUTH AND EMILY

                       EMILY
Let's just say, motherhood wasn't a natural fit. Trying isn't
the same as doing.
                (waiting for a response)
I think it's time we talk about Daniel staying here
permanently.

                        RUTH
                (now pacing)
I don't understand. Empty nest syndrome? He's my—

                       EMILY
I still talk to Bernadette Fuller.
                (after Ruth makes an exasperated noise)
She did go to our school and—

                        RUTH
Well before we did, and she escaped Reading as soon as
she could.

EMILY
As did you. I still talk to Bernadette, and she talks
to…everyone.

Ruth spells out "Roman" with the refrigerator magnets.

RUTH
By everyone you mean Cindy Drinkwater.

EMILY
Whoever. I know what's going on.

In a sudden motion, Ruth mixes up the letter magnets.

RUTH
Good, because I sure don't. Why don't you fill me in, sis?
Everyone else seems to enjoy enumerating my sins, real
and imagined, so you just jump in whenever your cold,
little heart desires. You hounded Charlie right into his…

A few moments of silence ensue. Emily's eyes fill up.

EMILY
You have no right.

RUTH
I don't. You're right. I'm sorry. I know you and Charlie
were the real deal. You had what I never had, what I'll
probably never have. I was just saying you talk a lot.

EMILY
Yeah, well, it runs in the family.

RUTH
And you don't have a small heart, Em. You're not the
Grinch.

EMILY
No, I'm not. I'm just the bad guy because I have to tell it
the way it is. You can't just tap your heels together three
times, then wake up and it's all better.

RUTH
I just want to speak to my son.

EMILY

Well, he doesn't want to speak to you, at least not right now. Maybe when some time passes.

Emily lowers the phone and tilts her head as if listening for something. She looks down the hall and sees Danny's door is closed. When *Moondance* begins, she seems satisfied.

RUTH

Tell me something about him, Em. Give me something.

EMILY

(sighing)
Well, he listens to a lot of music.

RUTH

Nothing new there.

EMILY

No, it's different. He's got Charlie's old turntable, and he plays records every chance he gets. He barely watches any television—he's only allowed two hours a day max anyway—but it's just records for Daniel.

RUTH

Vinyl records?

EMILY

He doesn't bother much with CDs or music from the computer. He's so into vinyl that when I had to punish...when he did something he shouldn't, I didn't ground him—he doesn't go out much anyway—or give him extra chores. I just took the turntable away for a couple of days. Did the trick.

RUTH

What does he...what does he listen to?

EMILY

Oh, Charlie's old stuff. '50s, '60s music mostly. Some '70s, I guess. There's one record he keeps playing over and over: *Moondance*. I know it by—

                    RUTH
Van Morrison?

                    EMILY
He asked me if there was any more. Only Daniel called
him Van the Man. Just like Charlie did.

EMILY'S HOUSE – DANNY'S ROOM

Occurs simultaneously with overlapping phone conversation:

Danny succeeds in breaking the Lady Bic cartridge that houses the razor.
He brushes the pink pieces into his book bag and runs his thumb across the
razor's edge, drawing blood. He sticks his thumb in his mouth

INTERCUT BETWEEN RUTH AND EMILY

                    RUTH
That's great! At his age, I liked the old stuff too. Old R&B
especially, remember? But, God, I was also so heavy into
Nirvana and—
                    EMILY
Terrific. Maybe when he finally wants to talk to you, you
can go get your tongues pierced together.

                    RUTH
When did you start hating me, Em? When I left Reading?
When I beat you in that fourth grade spelling bee? Tell me,
because I don't understand. Never did. Give me a hint.
Because you stayed in Podunk, Pennsylvania and I
escaped? Because Charlie died, and I have this perfect life
with a perfect husband? Tell me, Em.

                    EMILY
I don't hate you, Ruth. I don't know you well enough to
hate you. Not anymore. No, the question is: when did you
stop loving yourself?

Ruth stares at her distorted reflection in the stainless steel tea kettle.

                    RUTH
                (after a beat, quietly)
I'm not sure.

Ruth hangs up. Emily gently returns the receiver. Both women stare at the phone. Ruth furiously picks it up again and dials her sister back. Emily massages her temples for a few rings before she picks it up.

> RUTH (CONT'D)
> Took you long enough. I know you were sitting right—

> EMILY
> Some of us have things—

> RUTH
> Don't you think I did those same things—for years—for Danny?

> EMILY
> (sternly)
> Daniel belongs here. For how long, I don't know, but for a while. The newspaper article… It didn't help; it made things worse, worse than you know. Mondauk County is toxic for Daniel. He needs a new place just to be.

> RUTH
> (defeated with a hint of relief)
> No two ways.

> EMILY
> The interview. How could you? What were you thinking? Didn't you—
> (beat as Emily pulls herself together)
> Be sure of this: Daniel was raped. This is incontrovertible. That whore.

> RUTH
> No. Two ways.

The women hang up.

EMILY'S HOUSE – DANNY'S ROOM

What happens below occurs after Ruth's last words:

Danny sits at his desk with his sleeve rolled up, using the razor to make a second linear, parallel cut on his forearm. The first cut is fresh. But this is not a suicide attempt. These are the marks of a fledgling cutter.

EXT. RUTH'S HOUSE – DAY

Ruth walks out of her house to her car and discovers that all four of her tires have been slashed and eggs have been smashed on her windshield.

> RUTH
> Fuck it. She knows how. She did it. She knows.
> (looking at her watch)
> Time to draft Marcie for some recon—after a walk apparently.

EXT. MONDAUK MANOR PARK – DAY

Marcie, in pink jogging clothes and a winter coat, attempts some absurd-looking stretches by a war memorial. Ruth waits by a park sign until she is sure Marcie is alone.

> RUTH
> (approaching Marcie)
> I don't want to scare you.

> MARCIE
> (jumping)
> Well, you did! Heavens!
> (putting on mittens)
> The Walk and Talk Club. Not my idea, I don't mind saying—Cindy's—but I was outvoted. I didn't want to tell you especially after the Bookends and Bookmarks mess.

> RUTH
> I don't care.

> MARCIE
> You'd be a wonderful addition, of course. Look at your body.

> RUTH
> I don't care.

> MARCIE
> If I had your body—

                    RUTH

You wouldn't know want to do with it. Come to think of
it, *I* don't know what to do with it.

                    MARCIE
              (looking around nervously and
                whispering)
They'll be here soon.

                    RUTH

Still apathetic.

                    MARCIE

You're ill? You look tired.

                    RUTH

No—I don't care.

                    MARCIE

Oh, well, I do.

                    RUTH
              (in a gentler tone)
I know you do. I just need some information.

                    MARCIE

I'm sorry. I'm not sure what you want, but I'm pretty sure
I can't help.

                    RUTH

Maybe not. But Harold can.

                    MARCIE
              (taken aback)
My Harold?

                    RUTH

The very same. I just need some information—then a ride,
if you have time. Up and back. My car's out of
commission.
              (when she sees Marcie begin to shake
                her head)
You may not approve of me or even like me anymore,
Marcie, but you owe me something for all the bird

watching opportunities our little town's latest tragedy has afforded you. You at least owe me a ride.

They both hear a group of gabby women approaching. Marcie nods and mouths "okay."

                    RUTH (CONT'D)
      You're a pip.

Ruth turns and exits through some bushes as Cindy Drinkwater and friends approach.

                    CINDY
      And who was that?

                    MARCIE
      Who? Her? Nobody. Just lost is all.

                    CINDY
      Some people are just so stupid.

INT./EXT. PHIL'S CAR – NIGHT

Parked, Phil sits in the driver's seat while Jewels gives him a blowjob. Red glitter is everywhere. Phil reaches behind the seat and retrieves the gun. He points it at Jewels' bobbing head but never actually touches her with it. Jewels comes up for air, and she is neither surprised nor disturbed when she sees the gun, just curious.

                    JEWELS
      What are you doing?

                    PHIL
      Practicin'. Gun to her head, like she said.

He pushes her head down. A few seconds later, she comes back up.

                    JEWELS
      Houston, do we have a problem here? You skip your Wheaties this morning?

Phil tries to push her head down again, but she resists.

                    JEWELS (CONT'D)
I had a semester of college, you know. Mondauk County
Community College. Had a psychology course there. I
know, for instance, that a gun is a substitute for a cock. I
also know—

Phil shoves the barrel of the gun into her mouth. She begins to cry, and he
licks her running mascara. In quick succession, he removes the gun, leans
over to open the passenger door, and throws a crumpled bill at Jewels
before pushing her out.

                    JEWELS (CONT'D)
                (on the ground)
Twenty for sucking your cocktail weenie? Are you out of
your fucking—

Phil peels away without shutting the passenger door.

INT. MARCIE'S STATION WAGON – DAY

Marcie, wearing what looks like a teapot cozy on her head, and Ruth, with
large purple bags under her eyes, sit in an idling car outside the Blue Comet.
In the passenger seat, Ruth alternately clutches her purse and worries the
zipper on her bland, unfashionable winter coat. She keeps her gaze on the
front door of the Comet.

                    MARCIE
You want me to just drop you off. The other day you
said—

                    RUTH
I know what I'm doing.

                    MARCIE
On Sunday, Father Dave told us—

                    RUTH
I don't even have to guess what Father Dave said. Big
sermon fan.

                    MARCIE
                (awkwardly attempting to be sly)
But Deacon Romeo…

RUTH

Roman. His name is...stop this already. You know his name. And he's not a deacon. Not yet.

MARCIE

Mr. Roman then. Addie Mae—kidding of course—called him a pretty young thing, but then Cindy said he's *your* pretty young—

RUTH

Cindy Drinkwater needs to tend to her own backyard. It's pretty common knowledge that her husband has stuck his poker into more than one furnace.

MARCIE

Ruth! I never!

RUTH

No. You probably haven't.
(beat)
And why is that, Marcie? Because you and your prayer circle live your lives like the boy in the plastic bubble? Is that why the NPR crowd, the Super Catholics, the poinsettia-tending, most holy members of the Jane-Austin-Makes-Me-Wet-If–I-Use-A-Lubricant-Change-of-Life Book Club can't tell a comedy from a tragedy, a life-changing event from an old episode of Oprah? Christ, the one where she gave away new cars to everyone in the audience and then patted her own back fat must have made the Walk and Talk Club's collective nipples hard.

MARCIE

I don't know what...that was a moving...Oprah had the Angel Network.

RUTH

(looking at Marcie for the first time)
Two bullet points. Take 'em back to the coven. I'm sure the back fence yakety yak crew's already chewed 'em to the nubs anyhow. My Danny, my boy, my only...my son was sexually...no, he had sex. A teacher had sex with my Danny. Everybody knows that. And, yes, I just said boy, as in *my* boy, but Danny is young man, and my opinions on the difference—among other issues—are what got me in

Dutch with the local moral superiors. Is fifteen—sixteen in a couple of days—a *boy*? I'm not stupid, but what it comes down to is this: when is something not what it is? That's what I dared to ask. So, yes, Danny is "away," living with my sister in Reading, finishing up school far from the local rags and the likes of you, me, and Cindy Drinkwater, and he probably isn't coming back. That's one. Here comes bullet point two. Hold onto your Depends. I. Did not. Have sex. With Roman. But...here's the real morsel you can run back to the yentas with: I think I want to.

> MARCIE
> (shocked but pleased)
Ruth!

> RUTH
> (mocking her friend)
Marcie!
> (gentler)
I want to. I just don't know how.
> (looking up at the Blue Comet sign)
She's on shift now? You're sure?

> MARCIE
My Harold, he's not one for tap rooms, but he and Lucas from down the plant meet here for lunch sometimes—I don't know how you knew that—and he said she was tending bar when he went in today, so she should still be on. Harold came home from lunch an hour ago.

> RUTH
> (giving Marcie a look)
Lunch—right. I bet a lot of retired husbands have lunch "sometimes" in a—
> (trying to be good, focusing)
I could have just called, but I know they wouldn't have told me if she was there, and if I just showed up and she wasn't on, she might not come back. And I *really* think knocking on her front door might be pushing it. It's safer for all involved if this happens in public.

> MARCIE
> (growing anxious)
Uh-huh. Say, you don't have a gun or...

Ruth makes her fingers into the shape of a gun.

> RUTH
>
> Shucks. Must have left my real phallic symbol at your last
> book burning.

> MARCIE
>
> You know they have to wear all black in there. The
> women. Waitresses and what not. And they have to wear a
> splash of red. A red scarf. A red belt. Something red. My
> Harold, he says it has something to do with—

> RUTH
>
> Their menstrual cycles? I appreciate the ride, Marcie.
> I appreciate the ride, Marcie. I really do. I'll call a cab or
> take the bus back.

> MARCIE
>
> But—

> RUTH
>
> You work on that butt, Marcie, and your Harold might
> stop tinkering with his toy trains long enough to hop on
> your caboose again.

EXT./INT. THE BLUE COMET – DAY

Ruth gets out of the station wagon and shuts the door. As she fixes her
hair, she stares in an accusatory manner at her reflection in the Blue
Comet's window. When she enters the bar, she climbs onto a stool at the
end nearest the door. She does not remove her jacket.

Behind the bar, Lisa Ann washes glasses in a sink. The lunch crowd has
gone and the only other people sitting at the bar are Frank, Oreo, and
Rocco, all visibly intoxicated. Frank takes out his uppers, drops them into
his old fashioned glass, and grins at Ruth.

> LISA ANN
>
> You keep those teeth in, Frank, or Nicky'll make sure you
> swallow 'em.

Lisa Ann approaches Ruth and tosses down a cardboard coaster and a
napkin without really looking at her, her eyes on Frank.

LISA ANN (CONT'D)
(adjusting her red cloth choker)
What can I get you?

Ruth doesn't answer but reaches into her purse. Lisa Ann turns her head as Nicky comes through the basement door and approaches the bar.

FRANK
(slurring)
I'll buy the fair lady a drink. Spare no tiny umbrellas.

NICKY
(placing his hands on Frank's shoulders)
Another word, Henry Higgins, and I'll eighty-six you.
Swear to God. Leave the lady be.
(wiggling his pinky finger)
You ain't got dick to work with anyhow.

LISA ANN
(to Nicky)
I got it.

NICKY
We'll see.

LISA ANN
(turning to Ruth)
You need to see the lunch menu? We have sand—

Ruth slides a photograph across the bar. In the picture, Ruth and a young towheaded boy in a baseball uniform grin for the camera in a batter's cage. Lisa Ann takes the photo, looks at Ruth, and places the picture back on the bar with care.

NICKY
(realizing the identity of his new
customer)
Now, Ruth, we don't need any trouble. Why don't I just call Phil?

RUTH
Phil's gone, Nicky. You'll need a new bowling team member.

NICKY
Gone? Gone as in…

RUTH
(singing)
"Hit the road, Jack, and don't you come back no more, no more, no more, no more."

NICKY
You finally threw him out?

RUTH
(inscrutable)
No—I just like the song. But husband *is* gone. Husband took powder.

Nicky backs away, mumbling an apology. The two women stare at one another. Ruth remains unreadable. Lisa Ann looks terrified, but she is the one to break the silence.

LISA ANN
I thought I was in love.

Ruth sits up straight and listens with rapt attention.

LISA ANN (CONT'D)
It wasn't right, I know. Of that, there's little doubt. I was more than irresponsible. I never meant to hurt anyone, least of all…your family. Honestly, I know there's something wrong with me, but I don't have a thing for… I can't teach. I have court-mandated therapy, unannounced probation checks, and my picture on the Megan's Law website, and I'm sure you think that's not enough, Ruth. It wouldn't be enough for me. If I could take it all back—

RUTH
(growing more intense as she speaks)
Would you? Danny called it love too. If you were in love with my son, if you were *really* in love with your fifteen-year-old student, would you take it back—even in your heart? Would you not have taken his virginity? Would you not have made your secretly estranged husband seem like a cuckold? Would you not have made yourself an object of

ridicule, a registered sex offender in a town with over fifteen churches?
                    (beat)
If it *was* love...not your Sandra Bullock, Meg Ryan meet-cute kind of movie love, but the kind that pierces you, marks you, makes a Cain out of what was only an Abel, wouldn't you climb the highest mountains, swim the seven seas, write his name all over your notebooks? If it was *real* love—forget that Danny was underage, forget that for a minute, forget about possibly going to prison, which you somehow managed to avoid—wouldn't you put it all on the line? Your teaching career, your friends probably, your freedom? Wouldn't you do just about anything you could and some things you probably shouldn't to be able to wake up next to the one person who makes you want to take your next breath and who gives that breath meaning? What would you sacrifice to watch that person sleep, to have that person put his legs in your lap while he watches the game, to have him so deep inside you, you wonder if you'll ever be able to walk again? If it was love, Lisa Ann, I ask you: wouldn't you sacrifice everything?

                    LISA ANN
          (after a couple of beats, quietly)
I did.

Neither woman speaks for a few seconds. Frank belches and Lisa Ann pours him a new drink. Oreo slides a cookie to Ruth. When Lisa Ann turns her attention back to Danny's mother, Ruth places her hand over the bartender's. Lisa Ann doesn't flinch. Nicky watches intently from the far side of the bar.

                    RUTH
Teach me.

                    LISA ANN
What?

                    RUTH
Teach me how you did it.

                    LISA ANN
The seminarian.

(when Ruth doesn't respond)
Small town. Loose lips sink ships.

RUTH

I want to throw it all away. I mean, most of it is gone anyhow. I'm ready.

LISA ANN

Is he?

RUTH

Doesn't matter. Was Danny?

LISA ANN
(bowing her head a little)
I thought so, but I don't really know. Not anymore.
(beat)
With Roman, you're going up against… I'm not one of them, but some would say you could lose more than you bargained for, Ruth.

RUTH

My soul? Too late. So will you teach me? Will you show me how to let go?

FRANK
Narcissist Central, please hold.

LISA ANN

It's a process, then it just happens: you're in the air before you realize you jumped, and you jumped because you had no other choice by then. Lose a lot of blood before that point though. There's no textbook, no map, no Bible.

RUTH

Show me using a coloring book, I don't care. Just tell me how you were able to do it. Tell me that much at least. 'Cause I'm lost here.

LISA ANN
(after a beat)
Nicky—need a barback for the rest of my shift? Ruth can fill in.

Nicky appears relieved that the confrontation didn't escalate but quickly looks away.

> NICKY
> (nonchalantly)
> What the fuck, it's only a buck.

Lisa Ann takes off her red choker and tosses it to Ruth.

> LISA ANN
> So let's throw it all away then.

> RUTH
> All of it.

> LISA ANN
> What else is there?

> RUTH
> Nothing.

INT. DISC/CONNECTION – NIGHT

An independent record store. The music is loud. The incense smoke is thick. A couple of kids in black concert t-shirts huddle around a pair of headphones, while a few male just-from-work professional types peruse the racks. A girl with pink hair, a pierced septum, and a tattoo on her arm glares at Ruth when she catches the older woman looking at her.

Ruth passes the vinyl racks and instead cruises the CD browsers, stopping at the M's. Once she finds the Van Morrison CDs, she starts creating a large pile.

> RECORD STORE CLERK
> Can I help you with that?

> RUTH
> Do you have any more Van the Man?

> RECORD STORE CLERK
> I'll check in the back.

RUTH

That would be great, thanks. I'm going to tell the cab to wait another sec. Oh, and do you know if there's a UPS store around here that's still open?

INT. LISA ANN'S HOUSE – LIVING ROOM – NIGHT (DUSK)

LISA ANN
(on the phone)
I'm really sorry I put you through all this, Paul.

PAUL (V.O.)
What can I do? I want to kill you, but I'm still in love with you, so I can't.

Lisa Ann laughs.

PAUL (V.O. CONT'D)
As long as you're not hanging upside down, I'm okay.

LISA ANN
Glad to hear it. But have you changed your mind? Are you saying I'm like Cassiopeia after all? A sexual bully?

PAUL (V.O.)
No, but people want to punish you just the same.

INT. RUTH'S HOUSE – KITCHEN – NIGHT

Ruth slices cheese. A box of crackers sits on the table. Somewhat loud rock'n'roll emanates from the dining room. The phone rings.

RUTH
Hello? Yes?
(listening intently)
Oh, hey. I'm sorry, you'll have to speak up. I'm reliving my childhood.
(beat)
Yeah, but I'm leaving out the prom.
(laughing then listening)
Yep, tonight. We're still on. If you don't come over, I'll have to eat all this cheese by myself. I don't want to be

found with the stereo turned up to eleven, overdosed on
Brie and Gouda.
(beat)
No, but use the backdoor if you want.

INT. LISA ANN'S HOUSE – LIVING ROOM – NIGHT

LISA ANN
(on the phone)
I'd rather walk through the front.

INT. RUTH'S HOUSE – KITCHEN – NIGHT

RUTH
(smiling)
I'd rather you did too.
(beat)
Okay, see you then.

After hanging up, Ruth cranks the volume and, without a hint of irony,
sings the chorus into a wooden spoon accompanied by all the appropriate
rock star moves.

RUTH (CONT'D)
"Yeah I'm free! Free fallin'!"

INT. EMILY'S HOUSE – DANNY'S ROOM – NIGHT

Danny does his homework next to an old computer and a lamp with a
Reading Phillies shade, new additions to his desk.

EMILY (O.S.)
(knocking)
Can I come in?

Danny gets up and opens the door. Emily hands two packages to her
nephew.

EMILY (CONT'D)
Well, young man, your birthday came a day early it
seems—and you thought it was terrible to have a

Christmas Eve birthday. This one is from your mom. The other one... Well, I'll leave you to it. Remember: we're having your cake tonight because we're going to Aunt Enid's before Midnight Mass tomorrow.

Emily departs, closing the door behind her. Danny studies the packages—it is obvious that they'd been opened and re-taped—and shakes his head.

He sits on the bed and opens the box Emily indicated was from his mom. He digs through the packing peanuts and removes the bubblewrap to reveal sixteen Van Morrison CDs, which prompts a cry of delight.

He goes through them quickly and finds *Moondance*. A smile plays across his lips until he glances at his milk crate of vinyl on the floor, and his face hardens. He opens the card; there are just two handwritten words: "Love Me"—no comma. He shoves the *Moondance* CD beneath his pillow and dumps the rest of the discs and the card into the wastebasket.

Returning to his bed, he contemplates the second box. There is no return address. He shakes it gently. No sound. He opens it with care but then plunges his hands into a wad of tissue paper—and emerges with Casey's jeff cap, the brim slightly singed. Danny's face is swallowed in a look of pleasure.

He discovers a small envelope pinned to the hat. Inside is a single slip of paper: an e-mail address. He rushes to the computer and begins typing.

INT. EMILY'S HOUSE – UPSTAIRS HALLWAY – NIGHT

Emily leans against the wall, a smile lightening her usually grim visage, as she listens to the clack of the keys.

INT. PHIL'S CAR – NIGHT

Slouched down, an intoxicated Phil watches Lisa Ann leave her house, as he rubs the gun against his crotch. When Lisa Ann's car pulls away, Phil starts his and follows.

INT. MARCIE'S HOUSE – LIVING ROOM – NIGHT

Marcie watches Phil's car follow Lisa Ann's through her binoculars.

                    MARCIE
        This isn't going to end well.

                    HAROLD
            (tinkering with his trains)
    Can the Greek chorus stop portending long enough to
    hand me that little wrench there?

INT. RUTH'S HOUSE – KITCHEN – NIGHT

Ruth begins filling the tea kettle with water when the phone rings. A Van
Morrison CD plays at a medium volume in the dining room.

                    RUTH
        Hello?

                    DANNY (V.O.)
        Mom?

                    RUTH
            (stunned but elated)
        Danny?

INT. EMILY'S HOUSE – EMILY'S ROOM – NIGHT

                    RUTH (V.O.)
        I was going to call you tomorrow for your birthday.

                    DANNY
        Thank you for the box. How did you know I liked—

INTERCUT BETWEEN RUTH AND DANNY

                    RUTH
        Would you believe lucky guess?

Danny's face darkens, but the anger is fleeting.

                    RUTH (CONT'D)
        Danny, are you still—

DANNY

Mom, I just wanted to say—

RUTH

Me too, kiddo. Right back at ya.

Danny is momentarily annoyed. "I love you" wasn't what he was going to say.

DANNY
(after a couple of beats)
Mom, have you ever been in love?

RUTH
(hesitantly)
Well, your father…when we were—

DANNY

No, I mean *really* in love. Like it was always there, but one day it just kind of snuck up on you.

RUTH
(tip-toeing)
Like with Mrs.—like with Lisa Ann?

DANNY

No, not—

Ruth takes a distressed copy of *Dazzler* from the top of the fridge.

RUTH

Yes. Yes, I've really been in love.

DANNY
(picking up the jeff cap)
Isn't it the greatest feeling in the world when you find out?

RUTH
(bewildered but smiling)
Yes. Yes it is.
(as she hastily replaces the comic)
Is there something you want to tell—

                              DANNY
              You'll call me tomorrow for my birthday?

                               RUTH
                        (too enthusiastically)
              You bet!

                              DANNY
                             (wincing)
              Maybe even come visit soon?

                               RUTH
              Oh, yes! You just let me know—

                              DANNY
              I have to go now. Bye.

                               RUTH
              Oh, okay. I love…
                        (after the line goes dead)
              …you, Danny. No matter what. And I can always imagine
              the "what."

INT. PHIL'S CAR – NIGHT

A befuddled Phil watches Lisa Ann slow down on his street, as if looking
for an address number, and finally pull up in front of his house. Some of
the neighboring houses have Christmas lights up but not the St. Clairs'. Phil
parks a couple of cars down, as Lisa Ann walks up the steps of his house.
There is a furious yet dazed look on his face.

INT. RUTH'S HOUSE – LIVING ROOM – NIGHT

The doorbell rings and Ruth invites Lisa Ann into the house. Somewhere
down the block, carolers are singing. After looking at each other for a
moment, the two women catch their reflection in the entranceway mirror
and grin.

INT. RUTH'S HOUSE – KITCHEN – NIGHT

Lisa Ann takes a seat at the far end of the table. Van Morrison is still playing on the stereo. The blinds are open, and the neighbors' blinking Christmas lights tint the glass.

>   LISA ANN
> Good taste in music.

>   RUTH
> I get it from my son. Wine or beer or coffee?

>   LISA ANN
> I would love some tea.

>   RUTH
> A woman after my own heart.

Ruth places the kettle on the burner but doesn't light it. The saucepan goes next to it. The carolers can be heard just beneath Van Morrison. It sounds like a large group.

>   LISA ANN
> Carolers. You don't see that very often. Very Currier and
> Ives.

>   RUTH
> They'll be knocking soon—unless they plan on avoiding
> this house of ill repute. Don't you know? After Vatican
> City, the town of Mondauk Proper is the Jesus capitol of
> the world. Just ask Cindy Drinkwater. But forgive my
> cynicism, please. The carolers do sound pretty if you like
> that sort of thing.

>   LISA ANN
> You're just wound up. You have a perfectly nice
> bawdyhouse. But I have to ask: what's with the empty
> saucepan? Are we reducing a soup later?

>   RUTH
> Ah, the saucepan. Story goes: my mother was expecting a
> gentleman caller. The kettle whistle went off, drowning out
> the doorbell, so she began...

EXT. RUTH'S HOUSE – NIGHT

Careful to stay in the shadows, Phil stands on decorative bricks to watch the women through the kitchen windows. His hands become two fists, and his anger is such that the continuing conversation inside slowly becomes audible only after a long pull from his flask.

> RUTH
> (heard through the windows, in
> progress)
> ...sounds which attracted *another* man, my father, who put the ceramic teapot back together.

INT. RUTH'S HOUSE – KITCHEN – NIGHT

> LISA ANN
> Your father sounds like a nice man.

> RUTH
> He wasn't. He was vicious, a drunk, always scheming, but even a short con requires you to be sober enough to remember the grift. Turns out the teapot hadn't been as broken as he was. Speaking of degenerates, how do you know Phil?

> LISA ANN
> (anxious to change the subject)
> The saucepan?

She looks towards the windows as if she saw something outside. Ruth doesn't notice.

> RUTH
> When I was young and the booze had just taken firm hold of my father or vice versa, my mother put away her tea kettle for good and from then on only made tea—masala chai—in a saucepan. No whistle to contend with. Now, Chaiwalas in India use tons of sugar in their chai and so did my mother. Could be a fucking eye opener. Forget Count Chocula or Franken Berry. They were pussies compared to what my mother synthesized.

                    LISA ANN
Remember Boo Berry? I loved that time. Then it's like one
day someone steals all the fun stuff and leaves you with a
box of Tampax.

                    RUTH
One morning it was like, "Who took my Fruit Brute? And
what the hell do I need Motrin for?" Your childhood
ripped right out from under you.

EXT. RUTH'S HOUSE – NIGHT

As the women laugh, Phil undoes his belt and drops his pants.

                    RUTH
            (heard through the windows)
My mother told me quite bluntly that because of the
whistle she ended up marrying a souse instead of having
afternoon tea with a man of potential.

Phil begins masturbating furiously, cursing under his breath.

                RUTH (CONT'D)
Me? I don't have an excuse. I had some suitors but I could
never decide. Eventually there was one man standing.
Now he's half a man swaying.

When Phil sees the carolers across street, he moves deeper into the
shadows to continue his exertions and almost loses his balance. The
carolers provide his background music.

                RUTH (CONT'D)
                (in progress)
...and I swear, I thought I could see my father's handprint
painted in purple on her cheek, right after she bailed him
out. Did you try the Gouda?

Phil finishes, falls backwards onto the driveway, and knocks himself out, his
pants still down.

INT. RUTH'S HOUSE – KITCHEN – NIGHT

Lisa Ann reacts to the noise outside. Ruth is too caught up in her story to pay attention.

                    RUTH
          I guess the business with the saucepan started out as a way
          to honor my mom. I always take it out whenever I boil
          water for tea. It's just habit now. I long ago surrendered to
          the whims of the whistle. Too busy staring at my reflection
          in the saucepan to remember the ingredients for chai, I
          guess!
                    (laughing)
          I used to bug my mom: how will you know when the
          chai's done? There no whistle! "You have to watch it," she
          used to say. "But what if you walk out of the room?" I
          asked one afternoon. That's when I got the look. "Ruthie,"
          she said, "you just have to know it's there. If you 'hear' it,
          you're home."

                    LISA ANN
                    (sincerely)
          Wow.

                    RUTH
          "Hear what?" I asked. She told me, "You have a hall of
          mirrors up here," as she tapped my forehead, "and all that
          rushing from one mirror to another makes noise. You
          have to get out of the way of yourself to quiet things
          down, and when you do, you'll be able to hear the distant
          sound of boiling tea. You'll feel each moment as it goes
          past. Measuring the time for chai tea to boil will be the last
          of your concerns when you understand what each tick and
          bell *really* means."

                    LISA ANN
          Double wow. Goosebumps.

                    RUTH
          She also told me that I was blessed with an internal
          compass, and once I escaped the hall of mirrors, I'd find
          true north, and true north was always the direction home.
          Since a watch face can be used as a compass, it was all
          connected. If I could 'feel' the movement of time, then

that meant my mind was clear. Oh, shoot. I forgot to put the hummus out.

Lisa Ann glances towards the windows. Ruth notices this time.

> RUTH (CONT'D)
> Expecting someone?

> LISA ANN
> (thinking Ruth is referring to Danny)
> No, not—I swear. I just think…someone's following me.

> RUTH
> A rogue caroler? Look down, Lisa Ann: no ankle bracelet going off, playing your song. No elite police force fast-roping from helicopters.

> LISA ANN
> (ashamed)
> The judge acted as if… Did they tell you about my sentence?

> RUTH
> They did, but I didn't pay much attention.

> LISA ANN
> (eyeing the windows again)
> I think I'm violating my parole by being here.

> RUTH
> You're not.

EXT. RUTH'S HOUSE – NIGHT

A fat tabby cat runs across Phil's stomach as he starts to come to in the driveway. His ire returns as he stands, and he attempts to kick the cat. But his pants are still around his ankles, and he falls backwards a second time but doesn't lose consciousness. The cat watches from a distance. Phil pulls up his pants without standing.

> PHIL
> (to the cat)
> Come near me again, I'll wear you like a hat.

The tabby yawns and stretches.

INT. RUTH'S HOUSE – KITCHEN – NIGHT

> RUTH
> (lighting the burner)
> I didn't even put the kettle on, I'm so busy doing all the talking.

> LISA ANN
> Which is good. Otherwise we'd be just sitting here not eating the hummus.

> RUTH
> When Danny was little, I'd ask him if he could hear the distant sound of boiling tea whenever I brought out the saucepan, and one day he pinged it with his finger and sang, "Do you hear what I hear?"
> (ignoring Lisa Ann's schoolgirl giggle)
> For a few seconds, he stood there, cupping his ear, pretending to listen. Then he turned to me and said, in a most earnest voice, "Nope!" I chased him once around the living room, and every time he did this, which was often—I drink a lot of tea—he laughed that infectious laugh that only someone under the age of thirteen could manage.

A shadow staggers past the windows. Lisa Ann's eyes go wide.

> RUTH (CONT'D)
> But once my son became a teenager, he developed other diversions best practiced alone in his room. You'd think his extracurricular activity would have made him happy, but he became moody and talked less and less. Truth be told, though, I realized around the same time that I'd begun to resent that I couldn't just escape—not that I had anywhere to go. I missed the laughing boy, but I was just as scared that he'd return. And Phil? Well, I tried.

> LISA ANN
> Separating from Paul was the hardest decision I ever made. But I didn't do it because I didn't love him; I did it because he was in my way. I suppose that was my first step in throwing it all away, and I didn't even have anyone to

throw it all away for yet. But I hoped he was out there somewhere. This was before... Faith in the unknown wasn't as important as my willingness to explore it. Leaving Paul happened by degrees until finally I woke up one morning and tossed my marriage away for the opportunity to find, as your mother put it, true north. This is what you wanted to know about, right?

                    RUTH
              (nodding)
My case is a little different obviously. I'm tired of getting *out* of the way. I like the noise in my heart a hell of a lot better than the bedlam in my brain or the clamor and chaos of a drunk. Sure, I'm tossing away one set of problems for another, but I'm a big girl now and these are big girl choices.

                    LISA ANN
You don't want to put your life on hold for someone else's.
              (clarifying)
Phil's, I mean.

                    RUTH
              (sitting down)
You know what my son just asked me on the phone? He's been staying with my sister in Reading. After his arrest and everything—

                    LISA ANN
You don't have to explain.

                    RUTH
Good. Well, he asked me if I was ever *really* in love?

                    LISA ANN
What did you say?

                    RUTH
What did I say? I told him yes. I just didn't say with whom.

EXT. RUTH'S HOUSE – NIGHT

Phil dives into a neglected flower bed when a police car stops to shine a light up the driveway. When they leave, he brushes himself off, and the tabby begins to clean itself too. He throws a rock at the cat, and it runs away. Phil begins to mumble to himself as he peeks up the drive. Only the word "copycat" can be understood.

INT. RUTH'S HOUSE – KITCHEN – NIGHT

> LISA ANN
> It's like you're Wile E. Coyote.

> RUTH
> Oh, I always hated the Roadrunner cartoons.

> LISA ANN
> So did I. But hear me out. When you're in love, when it's the real deal, you're Wile E. Coyote and this...this *thing* you've been chasing your whole life is finally within reach, so you take that chance knowing that every time you've chased it before, it backfired, just like every time the Coyote chased the Roadrunner. But like Wile E., you can't help it, so you leap.

> RUTH
> And I thought my bruised knees were just fodder for bad blowjob jokes.

The two women stare at each other for a couple of beats.

> RUTH (CONT'D)
> Are we becoming friends?

> LISA ANN
> It's an unlikely pair.

> RUTH
> (with a lopsided smile)
> Then maybe you really don't know my husband. Unfortunately, he knows you, probably from the bar, and you're in his sights. Word to the wise.

LISA ANN
(looking away)
You shouldn't be allowed to get married until—

RUTH
(laughing)
Until you've already been married!
(beat)
And Mr. Kavanagh, how did he...?

LISA ANN
Handle all this? Surprisingly well. He's a true stoic, you
know. We were already separated when Danny and I...

RUTH
Stoicism is good. When did you realize your husband was
in your way?

LISA ANN
Paul and I were moving along on the fumes of the past:
old jokes, old lines, same positions, but we weren't the
same people. He's much older than me, and I was always
his eager pupil—until one day I wasn't, and that was it. I
decided I'd rather die violently chasing the Roadrunner
than end up being dead inside.
(beat)
I'm sorry I said "Danny and I" back there.

RUTH
You've avoided saying his name until now. But if we're
going to be friends, then we're just gonna have to dispense
with any tip-toeing. We're sitting here together because our
illogical choices made us the only people who could talk
about them logically. If that makes any sense.

LISA ANN
Narcissist Central.

RUTH
Yeah, well, fuck.

LISA ANN
So...the seminarian...Roman.

> RUTH
>
> And on with the show. Well, I didn't mention this at the bar because we were busy, but Roman has petitioned the diocese for a change of venue. Guess I almost scared the Jesus out of him. Almost. My feminine wiles are apparently a bit rusty. I did mention the last chance for a slow dance, right?

Lisa Ann jumps a little when she hears a thump outside.

> LISA ANN
>
> Did you hear that?

> RUTH
>
> Probably the neighbor's cat. Really fat tabby. Doesn't so much jump off fences as just lean over and fall off.

> LISA ANN
>
> Okay then. So what do you plan on doing about Roman's slow dance?

EXT. RUTH'S HOUSE – NIGHT

Phil watches the women through the windows again, mumbling through clenched teeth. Now only the words "cheating whore" can be made out.

Ruth gets up and sets out cups and saucers as well as sugar and lemon while she talks.

> RUTH
>
> (heard through the windows)
>
> If I were to do something, I'd have to act now. I doubt anyone's going to tell me what parish he'll finally be assigned to, and after he's been ordained and taken the vow…even I would think twice before messing with him then.

Phil moves around to the back of the house and tries the basement storm doors which give way after a couple of pulls. He stops mumbling and descends into the darkness.

INT. RUTH'S HOUSE – KITCHEN – NIGHT

Ruth stares briefly at a school photo of Danny hanging on the fridge and rearranges the letter magnets to spell "deep shit" as she speaks.

> RUTH
> But what's my plea? "You haven't tasted Heaven until you've had a woman staring forty in the face?" Maybe Roman wouldn't know from stretch marks. Look, I'm competing with God here. I'm definitely out of my weight class. Throwing it all away seems like my only chance.

> LISA ANN
> I'm your girl then. The key is not to be afraid of what you'll lose. In Buddhism, you let go of all attachments to achieve mindfulness. I did the opposite: I threw it all away for a chance at obsession. Once you've decided, it's no longer a matter of how hard. It's a matter of recognizing what you have to do to extricate yourself from your current entanglement and figuring out how to do it. From then on, you just hope the object of your affections is open to them because from the time you break free, it's an utter exposition of your once-caged soul and, by and large, ethics are temporarily relegated to the wastebasket.

INT. RUTH'S HOUSE – BASEMENT – NIGHT

Phil feels his way in the dark and begins creeping up the basement stairs. A step near the top issues a loud creak. He pauses but the women's conversation continues unabated. When he reaches the landing, he crouches, cracks the door, and absently rubs himself between his legs as he watches Ruth and Lisa Ann in the kitchen.

INT. RUTH'S HOUSE – KITCHEN – NIGHT

> RUTH
> (sitting again)
> What about you? What are you going to do now?

> LISA ANN
> I don't want you to worry, Ruth. I'm not going to pursue Danny or do anything… I was going to say crazy, but I've

already worn out that particular adjective. But to be honest, I don't know if I would've done anything different. As morally wrong as it was, I own what I did because what I did was real—inside, where it counts.

She pauses to listen to Van Morrison's epic "Take Me Back."

> LISA ANN (CONT'D)
> I'm pretty sure intentions don't get you off the karmic wheel, and they certainly don't make black white. You have no reason to, Ruth, but trust me: Danny and I, it's over. My next mortal sin awaits me down the road.

> RUTH
> (tenderly as Lisa Ann turns away)
> I think it's over for him too. The young move on faster than we do.

> LISA ANN
> (dabbing her eyes)
> I'm sure that's what Paul thinks about me and our marriage—except I'm not young, just younger than him.

> RUTH
> One thing's for sure: you can't keep on bartending at the Blue Comet full-time. The Comet's only a career for Nicky and the barflies. Teaching's out, so I was thinking: I know a woman in HR at County Hall. Her most recent assistant took a powder the second she said, "I do." Boring probably but rarely does anyone remove their teeth. As far as your conviction goes, well, this woman has a very liberal point of view. Interested?

Lisa Ann nods and says thank you just as the kettle begins to whistle. Ruth gets up and heads towards the stove but stops to pick up a fallen magnetic letter "p." She goes to the fridge and spells "pussy," then stands back and grins at Danny's picture. The sound of the kettle whistle gradually intensifies.

> RUTH (CONT'D)
> Loud, right? Better than waiting around for the dog whistle of boiling tea.

> LISA ANN
> Still, I can be standing right next to the stove sometimes and not even recognize the sound.

The whistle reaches full intensity: loud and intermittently shrill. The women laugh.

INT. RUTH'S HOUSE – BASEMENT – NIGHT

Startled by the kettle's fitful, piercing cries, Phil grabs the basement railing and reaches behind his back, under his shirt.

INT. RUTH'S HOUSE – KITCHEN – NIGHT

The sound of the carolers outside competes with the kettle whistle and Van Morrison as they get closer to Ruth's house.

> LISA ANN
> Think of the scandal. You and I hanging in your kitchen, ignoring the kettle.

> RUTH
> Yeah, Cindy Drinkwater would probably choke on her rosary.
> (beat)
> I have to ask this: was it worth it?

> LISA ANN
> (embarrassed but not looking away)
> Yes. For those few moments it was. And it was for this.

Lisa Ann stands, smiling. The two women meet halfway and embrace. Ruth's back is to the basement door; Lisa Ann's is to the stove, where the kettle continues to cry for attention. They let go of one another and are both laughing with tear-filled eyes as Phil bursts through the basement door with his gun raised.

Ruth begins to turn towards her husband, shouting something to him. A shot is fired. The last thing the bullet goes through before lodging in the wall is the kettle. Water sizzles as it spills through the hole into the flames. The whistle of the kettle is replaced with screaming.

Lisa Ann is standing between Phil and the stove. Her hands are over her stomach, and when she removes them, they are covered in blood.

> LISA ANN
> (showing her hands to Ruth)
> Oh, God, Ruth. You've been shot.

Lisa Ann falls. The screaming is replaced by Phil's high-pitched whine. He drops the gun and falls to his knees, exhausted. Ruth scrambles to Lisa Ann, but the teacher is dead. She picks up the gun and aims it at Phil. Lisa Ann's blood is all over her blouse and hands.

> RUTH
> (her voice shaking)
> You want to kill me, motherfucker? You can't even get that right, and I was standing right in front of you, but I bet I won't miss from here.

> PHIL
> Please, no. No, please don't, please don't. I'm beggin' you.
> (getting angry)
> What else do you want from me? Put down my gun, you...

Ruth places the barrel to his temple. Phil squeezes his eyes shut. He shimmers in red glitter. The last word of the line squeaks out.

> PHIL (CONT'D)
> ...bitch. No, no. I'm sorry. Please. I didn't mean—

Ruth cocks the gun, but something occurs to her as she glances at Lisa Ann's body.

> RUTH
> That wasn't meant for me, was it, Phil? The bullet?

Phil slowly shakes his head.

> RUTH (CONT'D)
> (as if shooting the gun)
> Pow.

With the revolver still at his temple, she reaches for the phone with her other hand and calls 911. The Van Morrison CD abruptly skips, then stops. Phil continues his wordless, high-pitched whining that merges...

EXT. RUTH'S HOUSE – NIGHT

...with the sound of sirens, as two police cars squeal to a halt in front of Ruth's house followed by an ambulance. A large group of carolers in robes stand watching.

INT. EMILY'S HOUSE – DANNY'S ROOM – NIGHT

As vinyl spins upon Danny's turntable, Van Morrison's "Take Me Back" picks up exactly from where it was cut off and continues to play beneath the action until the end.

INT. EMILY'S HOUSE – KITCHEN – NIGHT

Emily places the phone into the receiver and covers her face as she silently breaks down.

FLASHBACK – EMILY'S KITCHEN

A few minutes ago during Emily's phone call:

> RUTH (V.O.)
> (sobbing)
> Don't tell him, Em. Not today. Definitely not tomorrow.
> Promise me. Promise me that much.

Emily hangs up on her sister.

BACK TO PRESENT – EMILY'S KITCHEN

Emily forces herself to get it together. With shaky hands, she opens a cake box on the table.

INT. EMILY'S HOUSE – DANNY'S ROOM – NIGHT

Danny retrieves his mother's crumpled up card and sits at his desk. He stares at it, then inserts a comma between "Love" and "Me," and starts to roll up his sleeve.

> EMILY (O.S.)
> (yelling up the stairs)
> Danny! It's time!

Danny shoves a box of pens into a drawer, which he slams shut before exiting.

INT. EMILY'S HOUSE – KITCHEN – NIGHT

> RUTH (V.O.)
> Henry James wrote: "There are few hours in life more agreeable than the hour dedicated to the ceremony known as afternoon tea." I think what James was really saying was that it's the little things…

Emily watches Danny blow out candles on a birthday cake. When they turn out to be trick candles, he belly-laughs and keeps blowing. Finally he wets two fingertips and extinguishes a candle. He grins at Emily and flexes his arms like a superhero. Emily claps and grins back: he's a boy again. Danny quickly lowers his arms and adjusts his sleeves.

FLASHBACK – ASSUMPTION RECTORY LIBRARY – NIGHT

> RUTH (V.O. CONT'D)
> …like two hands touching or having an inside joke…

Roman takes Ruth's hand and gently pulls her back to her chair.

FLASHBACK – LISA ANN'S LIVING ROOM – NIGHT

> RUTH (V.O. CONT'D)
> …that puts the big things, like falling in love…

Lisa Ann runs her finger down a recent yearbook picture of Danny while on the phone.

FLASHBACK – POLICE STATION – NIGHT

> RUTH (V.O. CONT'D)
> …or raising a son…

Ruth and Danny exit the police station.

FLASHBACK – RUTH'S KITCHEN – NIGHT

> RUTH (V.O. CONT'D)
> …or making a new friend, into perspective.

Lisa Ann's blood is all over Ruth's blouse and hands.

FLASHBACK – EMILY'S HOUSE – DANNY'S ROOM – NIGHT

> RUTH (V.O. CONT'D)
> When a big thing is gone…

Danny dumps the CDs and card into the wastebasket.

FLASHBACK – RUTH'S KITCHEN – DAY

> RUTH (V.O. CONT'D)
> …it's all the little things that made up the big thing that you mourn: smells, jokes, snores.

A younger Danny pings the saucepan and sings, "Do you hear what I hear?" before running away, squealing as Ruth gives chase.

FLASHBACK – ASSUMPTION OF OUR LADY CHURCH – NIGHT

> RUTH (V.O. CONT'D)
> Your hand still seeks out another's that is no longer there…

Roman appears to be alone. He kneels in a pew, his forehead pressed into his tightly clasped hands. He shudders and his rosary swings. Father Dave looks on, then leaves.

FLASHBACK – RUTH'S KITCHEN – DAY

> RUTH (V.O. CONT'D)
> …and it takes forever for your brain to grasp the fact that it's impossible to tickle yourself.

Ruth sits at the kitchen table, violently paging through a *Dazzler* comic book. She rapidly finishes and throws it into the corner with the others.

BACK TO PRESENT – EMILY'S KITCHEN – NIGHT

> RUTH (V. O. CONT'D)
> It's like the sound of the last train pulling into a station. From your bed, all alone, late at night, its whistle, once the welcoming sound of a hello, becomes the loneliest sound in all the world.

The cake is gone. Sitting in front of Danny is a small pile of vinyl and balled up wrapping paper. He is beaming. When Emily turns away and starts cleaning up, Danny reaches into his lap and brings up Casey's jeff cap.

> RUTH (V.O. CONT'D)
> Maybe the distant sound of boiling tea was just my mother's way of escaping the whistle that had left her with doorbell regrets and ghostly wisps of what could-have-been.

Danny stares at the jeff cap for a moment or two, and when he realizes that Emily is watching, he places it on his head, holds it there, and starts posing. The sleeve of his shirt slides down, revealing a multitude of cuts. He quickly lowers his arm and fixes the sleeve. The jeff cap slides off his head and back into his lap.

> RUTH (V.O. CONT'D)
> Maybe there is no such thing as true north. How can we find our way home when we never really left and flight is nothing but a pipe dream? Even if our lives are made up of ticks and bells and the slamming of doors, it's the mundane whistle of a tea kettle or a train or a child we fear the most, for in it can hide a scream—and who can ever escape a scream?

It is unclear whether Emily has seen the cuts or if she is pretending for the moment that she hasn't. She puts on a kettle for tea as Danny continues to smile and laugh during an unheard conversation.

"Take Me Back" ends shortly after Ruth's voice-over finishes.

INT. RUTH'S HOUSE – UPSTAIRS BATHROOM – NIGHT

What occurs below plays out over the hiss of the turntable's needle being stuck in the playout groove.

Ruth, with spots of blood on her face, stares into the mirror as she raises lipstick to her mouth with a tremulous hand. But instead of applying the makeup, she draws an X on the mirror in two violent slashes and continues to stare. There is a soft knock on the door.

> DETECTIVE COTTEN (O.S.)
> Mrs. St. Clair, it's time to go.

Ruth slams the light switch off. In the glow of a night-light, she still seeks her face in the mirror. When she starts to cry, she slaps herself.

> RUTH
> (addressing her shadowy image)
> You're not a little girl anymore.
> (beat)
> I'll never let them make you a victim. I'll never make you
> feel like you did something bad, not if I—

INT. EMILY'S HOUSE – DANNY'S ROOM – NIGHT

Danny's hand removes the needle from the playout groove.

FADE OUT.

-END-

"And hollow, hollow, hollow all delight."

Alfred Lord Tennyson, *Idylls of the King*

About the Author.

Michael-Patrick Timothy Harrington was born in Philadelphia but now calls the small suburban town of Ambler, PA his home.

Michael-Patrick wrote his first short story in second grade and never looked back. He played bass in the band Zen Arcade when he was in college (the first time) and was the guitarist for Lola & the Shivers twelve years later. He was one of the primary songwriters in both groups.

At Holy Ghost Preparatory School, the author wrote for the literary magazine *The Torch*, which he renamed *Rhapsody* when he was the editor in his senior year. In the '90s, Michael-Patrick wrote for the music magazine *Rockpile*. His first assignment was to interview Patti Smith. He has also written press releases and promotional material for various businesses and organizations. The author currently maintains a blog on his web site.

Michael-Patrick opened a record store in the'90s, Disc/Connection. He published and largely wrote a monthly newsletter, *Back/Slash*, for the store's many club members. During the Disc/Connection years, he began a mail order company, UnderDog Mail Order, which still exists today as Mondauk Music. During the same time, Michael-Patrick founded Triquetra Records, an independent record label focusing on local music. Triquetra released nine albums in the late '90s and was involved with three others.

The author attended La Salle University but ultimately graduated magna cum laude from Arcadia University with a degree in English and Creative Writing.

The Distant Sound of Boiling Tea is Michael-Patrick's fifth book. It began as a writing assignment in the Play and Screenwriting Workshop at Arcadia and grew from there. Part of the work was performed at the Arcadia University Theater in 2010.

Michael-Patrick supports the following charity organizations:
National Multiple Sclerosis Society: www.nationalmssociety.org
Brookline Labrador Retriever Rescue: www.brooklinelabrescue.org

Contact the author at: michael@michaelpatrickharrington.com

www.michaelpatrickharrington.com

www.ingramcontent.com/pod-product-compliance
Lightning Source LLC
Chambersburg PA
CBHW060223180626
46813CB00007B/2940